Elijah Kellog

Lion Ben of Elm Island

Elijah Kellogg

Lion Ben of Elm Island

1st Edition | ISBN: 978-3-75234-730-2

Place of Publication: Frankfurt am Main, Germany

Year of Publication: 2020

Outlook Verlag GmbH, Germany.

Reproduction of the original.

LION BEN
OF
ELM ISLAND.

BY

REV. ELIJAH KELLOGG

PREFACE.

IF the writer ever tasted unalloyed happiness, it has been when exciting to manly effort a noble boy, whose nature responded to the impulse as a generous horse leaps under the pressure of the knee.

Hours and years thus spent have brought their own reward. The desire to meet a want not as yet fully satisfied, to impart pleasure, and, at the same time, inspire respect for labor, integrity, and every noble sentiment, has originated the stories contained in the "Elm Island Series," in which we shall endeavor to place before American youth the home life of those from whom they sprung; the boy life of those who grew up amid the exciting scenes and peculiar perils and enjoyments incident to frontier life, by sea and land; in fine, that type of character which has transformed a wilderness into a land of liberty and wealth, and replaced the log canoe of the pioneer by a commerce, the marvel of the age;—to the intent that, as insects take the color of the bark on which they feed, they also may learn to despise effeminacy and vice, and sympathize with, and emulate, the virtues they here find portrayed.

CHAPTER I.

ELM ISLAND.

IN one of the most beautiful of the many romantic spots on the rugged coast of Eastern Maine lived Captain Ben Rhines. The country was just emerging from the terrible struggle of the revolution, and the eastern part of the state had settled very slowly. The older portion of the inhabitants, now living in frame houses, had been born and passed their childhood in log camps.

Captain Rhines's house stood at the head of a little cove, on the western side of a large bay, formed by a sweep in the main shore on the one side, and a point on the other, called (from the name of its owner, Isaac Murch) "Uncle Isaac's Point."

A small stream, that carried a saw and grist mill, found an outlet at the head of it, while the milldam served the inhabitants for a bridge. A number of islands were scattered over the surface of the bay, some of them containing hundreds of acres; others, a mere patch of rock and turf, fringed with the white foam of the breakers.

At a distance of six miles, broad off at sea, in a north-westerly direction, lay an island, called Elm Island, deriving its name from the great numbers of that tree which grew on its southern end.

As we shall have a great deal to do with this island, it is necessary to be particular in the description of it. It was about three miles in length, rocks and all, by two in width, running north-east and south-west, and parallel to the main land. From the eastern side, Captain Rhines's house and the whole extent of the bay, and Uncle Isaac's Point, were visible. Nature seemed to have lavished her skill upon this secluded spot.

The island was formed by two ridges of rock forming the line of the shore, the intervening valley dividing the island nearly in the middle. These ridges sloped gradually, on their inner sides, into fertile swales of deep, strong soil. The shores were perpendicular, dropping plump down into the ocean, being in some places forty feet above the level of the water. They were rent and seamed by the frost and waves; and, in the crevices of the rocks, the spruce and birch trees thrust their roots, and, clinging to the face of the cliff, struggled for life with waves and tempests.

3

The island would have been well nigh inaccessible, had not nature provided on the south-western end a most remarkable harbor. The line of perpendicular cliffs on the north-west ran the whole length of the island, against which, even in calm weather, the ground-swell of the ocean eternally beat. The westerly ridge, which was covered with soil of a moderate depth, gradually sloped as it approached the south-western end, till it terminated in a broad space occupying the whole width between the outer cliffs, and gradually sloping to the water's edge. This portion of the island was bare of wood, and covered with green grass. The eastern ridge terminated in a long, broad point, covered with a growth of spruce trees, so dense that not a breath of wind could get through them, and, curving around, formed a beautiful cove, whose precipitous sides broke off the easterly sea and gales.

Into the head of this cove poured a brook, which, like a little boy, had a very small beginning. It came out from beneath the roots of two yellow birch trees that grew side by side in a little stream not more than two inches deep. As it ran on, it was joined by two other springs, that came out from the westerly ridge. The waters of these springs, together with the rains which slowly filtered through the forest, made quite a brook, which was never dry in the hottest weather.

At certain periods of the year the frost-fish and the smelts came up from the sea into the mouth of this brook. The cove, also, was full of flounders and minnows, eels and lobsters, and abounded in clams. The fish attracted the fish-hawks and herons, who filled the woods with their notes. Sometimes there would be ten blue herons' nests on one great beech. The fish-hawks attracted the eagles, who obtained their principal living by robbing the fish-hawks. The wild geese, coots, whistlers, brants, and sea-ducks also came there to drink. This was not the natural habitat of the large blue heron, their food not being found there to any great extent, as the shores were too bold, and the waters too deep; their favorite feeding grounds are the broad shallow coves, where they can wade into the water with their long legs, and catch little fish as they come up on the flood tide; but they prefer to go after their food, rather than abandon this secluded spot, where they are secure from all enemies, and where the tall trees afforded these shy birds such advantages for building their nests. As for the fish-hawks, who dive and take their food from the water, it was just the place for them.

There was also on the eastern side of the western ridge a swamp, a most solitary place, so thickly timbered with enormous hemlocks and firs, mixed with white cedar, that it was almost as dark as twilight at noonday. Here dwelt an innumerable multitude of herons, where they had bred undisturbed for ages. Much smaller than the great blue heron, they built their nests in the low firs and cedars; and as they fed upon frogs, grasshoppers, mice, tadpoles, and minnows, they were not obliged to leave the island for their food: they were perfectly at home and happy.

They belonged to that species called, by naturalists, *ardea nycticorax*. The inhabitants called them squawks and flying foxes, from the noise they made. Like all the heron tribe, they are extremely quick of hearing, and feed mostly in the morning and evening twilight, half asleep through the day among the branches of the firs, standing on one leg. They make shallow nests of sticks, and lay three or four green eggs. You may walk through their haunts: all is still as death, apparently not a heron on the island, while thousands of them are right over your head, and all around you, listening to every step you take, the slightest noise of which they will hear, when you do not notice it yourself. Crack goes a dry stick under your foot; you catch your toe under a spruce root, and tumble down; instantly the intense stillness of the woods is broken by a flapping of wings and rustling of branches, succeeded by quaw, quaw, squawk, squawk, producing a chorus almost deafening. The sound they emit, which is a union of growl, bark, and scream, comes from their throat with such suddenness, breaking upon the deep silence of the woods, like the whirr of the partridge, that it will make you jump, though you are prepared for it and accustomed to it. Then you will see them, after flying to a safe distance, light on the tips of the fir limbs, holding themselves up with their wings on the bending branch, like a bobolink on a spear of herds-grass, from which they will in an instant crawl down into the middle of the tree, sitting close to the trunk, where it is impossible to see them. You must therefore shoot them when they are on the wing, or at the moment they light.

They will bear a great deal of killing, and even make believe dead. I knew a boy once who shot four squawks, and after beating them with an iron ramrod, left them tied up in his pocket-handkerchief at the foot of a tree while he was clambering up after eggs: when he came down, two of them had crawled out of the handkerchief and run away. They will show fight, too, when they are wounded, bite and thrust with their bill, and scratch terribly with their claws. As if to compensate for the horrible noise they make, the full-grown male is a very handsome bird. The top of the head and back are green, the eyes a bright, flashing red, and just above them a little patch of pure white. The bill is black, the wings are light blue, the back part and sides of the neck lilac, shading on the front and breast to a cream color, and the legs yellow. From the back part of the head depend three feathers, white as snow and extremely delicate, rolled together, and as long as the neck.

The mouth of the little brook of which we have spoken was a very busy place when the fish-hawks were fishing, or carrying sticks to build their nests, and screaming with all their might, the herons fishing for minnows, squawks catching frogs, the wild geese making their peculiar noise, the sea-fowl diving, the ducks quacking, and the fish jumping from the water in schools. It shows how God provides for all his creatures, for though there are thousands of these islands scattered along the coast of Maine, on the smallest of them, and some that are mere rocks, you will find springs of living water.

On this island was a spring, that whenever the tide was in was six feet under water; but when the tide ebbed, there was the spring bubbling up in the white sand, as good fresh water as was ever drank.

Old Skipper Brown said he knew the time when it was a rod up the bank; that when he used to go fishing with his father, he had filled many a jug with water out of it; but the frost and the sea had undermined the bank and washed it away, till the tide came to flow over it.

There is another thing in relation to this little harbor, of great importance; for though the high rocks and the thick wood sheltered the little cove from all but the south and south-west winds, yet it would have been (at any rate the mouth of it) very much exposed to the whole sweep of the Atlantic waves in southerly gales; and though the cove was so winding that a vessel in the head of it could not be hurt by the sea, yet it would have been very hard going in, and impossible to get out in bad weather, had it not been for a provision of nature, of which I shall now speak, consisting of some ragged and outlying rocks.

One of these was called the White Bull, deriving its name from the peculiar hoarse roar which the sea made as it broke upon it, and also the white cliffs of which it was composed. It was a long granite ledge, perpendicular on the inside, and far above the reach of the highest waves. On the seaward side it ran off into irregular broken reefs, covered with kelp, the home of the rock cod and lobster, and the favorite resort of all the diving sea-fowl, who fed on the weeds growing on the bottom.

In the centre of these reefs was a large cove. Between this rock and the eastern point of the island was another, of similar shape, but smaller dimensions, called the Little Bull: they were connected by a reef running beneath the water, against which the sea broke, in storms, with great fury; and even in calm weather, from the ground swell of the ocean, it was white with the foaming breakers.

On the western side was a long, high, narrow island, called, from its shape, the "Junk of Pork," with deep water all around it, and covered with grass. The two ends of this island lapped by the western point of the White Bull and the western point of the main island, thus presenting a complete barrier against the sea. The whole space between the main land and these outlying rocks and islands was a beautiful harbor, the bottom of which was clay, and sand on top, thus affording an excellent hold to anchors.

There were two passages to go in and out, according as the wind might happen to be, with deep water close to the rocks. This harbor was a favorite resort of the fishermen, who came here to dig clams in the cove, and catch menhaden and herring for bait; they also stopped here in the afternoons to get water, and make a fire on the rocks, and take a cup of tea, before they went out to fish all night for hake; they also resorted to it in the morning to dress their fish and make a chowder, and lie under the shadow of the trees and sleep all the afternoon, that they might be ready to go out the next night.

The bottom of the cove on the White Bull was of granite, sloping gradually into deep water, and smooth as ice. Beneath this formation of granite was a blue rock of much softer texture than granite. The sea, in great storms, rolled the fragments of blue stone back and forth on this granite floor, and wore away and rounded the corners, making them of the shape of those you see in the pavements of the cities. The action of these stones for hundreds of years, on this granite floor, had worn holes in it as big as the mouth of a well, and two or three feet in depth. Sometimes a great square rock would get in one of them, too big for the summer winds to fling out, and the sea would roll it round in the hole all summer, wear the corners off, and then the December gales would wash it out. Among the quartz sand in the bottom of this cove you could pick up crystals that had been ground out of the rocks, from an eighth of an inch to an inch in diameter.

It was a glorious sight to behold, and one never to be forgotten, either in this world or the next, when the waves, which had been growing beneath the winter's gale the whole breadth of the Atlantic, came thundering in on these ragged rocks, breaking thirty feet high, pouring through the gaps between them, white foam on their summits and deep green beneath, and when a gleam of sunshine, breaking from a ragged cloud, flashed along their edges, displaying for a moment all the colors of the rainbow. But when in the outer cove of the White Bull the great wave came up, a quarter of a mile in length, bearing before it the pebbles, some weighing three hundred pounds, others not larger than a sparrow's egg, all alive and moving in the surf, and rolling over each other on the smooth granite bottom, how solemn to listen to that awful roar, like the voice of Almighty God!

Amid all this commotion, the little harbor, protected by its granite ramparts, was tranquil as a summer's lake. The surface of it was indeed flecked with the froth of the breakers that drifted in little bunches through the gaps of the rocks, and there was a slight movement caused by the last pulsation of some dying wave; but that was all, and way up in the cove there was no motion whatever.

It may be interesting as well as instructive, having the old traditions of the island to guide us, to consider the manner in which this picturesque and most useful harbor was formed.

Captain Rhines said his father told him, that when he was a boy (nearly seventy years before the date of our tale) these outer rocks were all connected with the main island. Between the eastern end of the island and the Little Bull, and between the Little Bull and the White Bull, was a strip of clay loam, covered with a growth of fir, hemlock, and spruce; and between the White Bull and the Junk of Pork, and the western point of the main island, were sand-spits mixed with stones, and salt grass growing on them. What is now the harbor was then a swamp, into which the brook and all the rain-water from the higher portions of the island drained. In the middle of this swamp was a pond, margined with alder bushes, cat-tail flags, and rotten logs. In high courses of tides the salt water came into it, and this brackish water bred myriads of mosquitos.

When people went on there, they had to pick a smooth time, and go right on the top of the tide, and haul their boat over a sand-spit into the swamp. It was impossible to land, or get away from there, when it was rough. Captain Rhines went on there once a gunning, in December, and had to stay a week. Having no axe to build a camp, he turned his boat bottom up to sleep under, and getting fire with his gun, cooked and ate sea-fowl; but he got awful tired of them.

He said, moreover, that the land on the outside kept caving off every spring when the frost came out, and falling into the sea, till there was only a little strip of land, with three old hemlocks upon it, left; and he used to pity them as they stood there shivering in the gale, their great roots sticking out drying in the wind, and dripping with salt spray, for he knew they were doomed, and must go.

At length there came a dreadful high tide and south-east gale; the sea broke in and swept the whole soil off, and in the course of ten years turned it into a clam bed. It was the greatest place to get clams, for a clam chowder, that ever was in the world. He said that it kept gradually scouring out and deepening, till it became a first-rate harbor.

This island was owned by a merchant of Boston, in whose employ Captain Rhines had sailed for many years, who gave him liberty to pasture it with sheep, as a recompense for taking care of and preventing squatters from plundering it of spars and timber. As sheep are very fond of sea-weed and

8

kelp, they would make a very good living on a place like this island, where most of our domestic animals would find pretty hard fare.

An island like this of which I have spoken is a very pretty spot to describe or visit; but I should like to ask my young readers if they think they could be happy in such a place, especially after they have enumerated with me the things, those we suppose to be living there would be deprived of, and which they often imagine they could not live without.

There was not a road on the island, nor a side-walk, only foot-paths; not a horse, a store, church, school-house, post-office, museum, or toy-shop; not a piano, nor any kind of musical instrument, except the grand diapason of the breakers; no circus, caravan, soldiers, nor fireworks; no confectionery nor ice-creams.

The island stood alone in the ocean; and though you could land at any time when you could get there, yet there were weeks together in winter, when, in case of sickness or death, not a boat could live to cross from the main land; they were completely shut out from all the rest of the world. But you say, perhaps, these people must have been very poor.

O, not at all. If you mean, by being poor, that they had not much money, or horses, or carriages, or rich dresses, and servants to wait on them, why, then they were poor; but if you mean by the term poor, such poverty as you see in the cities or in the large country towns, where you may see aged women in rags begging from door to door; children with their little bare feet as red as the pigeons' with the cold, picking the little bits of coal out of the ashes that are thrown out of the stores and houses; gathering pieces of hoops and chips around the wharves and warehouses to carry home to burn; with the tears running down their little cheeks, crying, "Please give me a cent to buy some bread,"—O, there was no such poverty as that there: they never knew what it was to want good wholesome food, and good coarse warm clothing to keep out the frost and snow.

"But how did they get it, if they had not much money to buy it?"

"Get it? Why, they worked for it; and if any one had called these island people beggars, they would have broken his head, or flung him overboard."

You may think as you like, my young friends; but people did live on this island, and were happy as the days are long, though they had their trials and "head flaws," as we all must.

CHAPTER II.

THE RHINES FAMILY.

In order that you may know all about them, we will resume the thread of our story, and trace the history of Captain Rhines and his family.

The captain was a strong-built, finely proportioned, "hard-a-weather" sailor, not a great deal the worse for wear, and seasoned by the suns and frosts of many climates. In early life he had experienced the bitter struggle with poverty.

His father came into the country when it was a wilderness, with nothing but a narrow axe, and strength to use it. His first crops being cut off by the frosts, they were compelled to live for months upon clams, and the leaves of beech trees boiled. There were no schools; and the parents, engaged in a desperate struggle for existence with famine and the Indians, were unable to instruct their children. Fishing vessels from Marblehead often anchored in the cove near the log camp, and little Ben, anxious to earn somewhat to aid his parents in their poverty, went as cook in one of these vessels when so small that some one had to hang on the pot for him. He was thus engaged for several summers, till big enough to go as boy in a coaster. During the winters, arrayed in buckskin breeches, Indian moccasons, and a coon-skin cap, he helped his father make staves, and hauled them to the landing on a hand-sled.

At nineteen years of age he went to Salem, and shipped in a brig bound to Havana, to load with sugar for Europe. He was then a tall, handsome, resolute boy as ever the sun shone upon, without a single vicious habit; for his parents, though poor, were religious, and had brought him up to hard work and the fear of God.

He was passionately fond of a gun and dogs, and what little leisure he ever had was spent in hunting and fowling. As respected his fitness for his position, he could "steer a good trick," had learned what little seamanship was to be obtained on board a fisherman and coaster, but he could not read, or even write his name.

The mate of the vessel conceived a liking for him the moment he came over the ship's side, and this good opinion increased upon acquaintance. They had been but a fortnight at sea, when he said to the captain, "That long-legged boy, who shipped for a green hand, will be as good a man as we have on board before we get into the English Channel; he will reeve studding-sail gear, already, quicker than any ordinary seaman. I liked the cut of his jib the moment I clapped eyes on him. If that boy lives he'll be master of a ship before many years."

"I hardly see how that can be," replied the captain, "for he can't write his own name."

"Can't write his own name! Why, that is impossible."

"At any rate he made his mark on the ship's articles, and he is the only one of the crew who did."

"Well," replied the mate, "I can't see through it; but he's in my watch, and I'll know more about it before twenty-four hours."

That night the mate went forward where Ben was keeping the lookout.

"Ben!"

"Ay, ay, sir."

"Where do you hail from?"

"Way down in the woods in Maine, Mr. Brown."

"What was you about there?"

"Fishing and coasting summers, and working in the woods in the winter."

"Why didn't you ship, then, for an ordinary seaman, and get more wages?"

"Because, sir, I was never in a square-rigged vessel before, and I didn't want to ship to do what I might not be able to perform."

"I see you made your 'mark' on the brig's articles. Were you never at school?"

"No, sir."

"Why not?"

"There's no such thing where I came from."

"Couldn't your parents read and write?"

"Yes, sir."

"Then why didn't they learn you themselves?"

"There were a good many of us, sir, and they were so put to it to raise enough to live on, and fight the Indians, they had no time for it."

The mate was a noble-hearted man; all his sympathies were touched at seeing so fine a young man prevented from rising by an ignorance that was no fault of his own. He took two or three turns across the deck, and at length said,—

"I tell you what it is, youngster: I'll say this much before your face or behind your back: you're just the best behaved boy, the quickest to learn your duty, and the most willing to do it, that I ever saw, and I've been following the sea for nearly thirty years; and before I'll see an American boy like you kept down by ignorance, I'll do as I'd be done by—turn schoolmaster, and teach you myself."

Mr. Brown was as good as his word. While the rest of the crew in their forenoon watch below were mending their clothes, telling long yarns, or playing cards, and when in port drinking and frolicking, Ben was learning to read and write, and putting his whole soul into it. He stuck to the vessel, and Mr. Brown stuck to him. When he shipped the next voyage as able seaman, he wrote his name in good fair hand.

They went to Charleston, South Carolina, to load with pitch, rice, and deer-skins, for Liverpool. The vessel was a long time completing her cargo, as it had to be picked up from the plantations. Ben improved the time to learn navigation. From Liverpool they went to Barbadoes. While lying there, the captain of the ship James Welch, of Boston, named after the principal owner, died. The mate taking charge of the ship, Ben, by Mr. Brown's recommendation, obtained the first mate's berth. He was now no longer Ben, but Mr. Rhines, and finally becoming master of the ship, continued in the employ of Mr. Welch as long as he followed the sea. He then married, built a house on the site of the old log camp, and surrounded it with fruit and shade trees, for, by travel and observation, he had acquired ideas of taste, beauty, and comfort, quite in advance of the times, or his neighbors. He then took his parents home to live with him, and made their last days happy.

Although he was compelled by necessity thus early to go to sea, he had a strong attachment to the soil, and would have devoted himself to its cultivation in middle life, had he not met with losses, which so much embarrassed him, that he was compelled to continue at sea to extricate himself.

Captain Rhines's fine house, nice furniture, and curiosities which he brought home from time to time, excited no heart-burnings among his neighbors, because they knew he had earned them by hard work, and did not think himself better than others on account of that.

Thus, when he became embarrassed, instead of saying, "Good enough for him," "He will have to leave off some of his quarter-deck airs now," everybody felt sorry for him, and told him so.

Indeed, everything about the Rhines family was pleasant, and excited cheerful emotions. The old house itself had a most comfortable, cosy look, as it lay in the very eye of the sun, with an orchard before it, green fields stretching along the water, sheltered on the north-west by high land and forest. The shores were fringed with thickets of beech and birch, branches of which, at high tide, almost touched the surface of the water.

Some houses are high and thin, resembling a sheet of gingerbread set on edge; they impress you with a painful feeling of insecurity, as though they might blow over. Such houses generally have all the windows abreast, so that when the curtains are up, and the blinds open, you can look right through them. They seem cold, cheerless, repellent; you shrug your shoulders and shiver as you look at them. But *this* house was large on the ground, and looked as if it grew there, with an ell and long shed running to the barn, a sunny door-yard, a spreading beech before the end door, with a great wood-pile under it, suggestive of rousing fires.

There was a row of Lombardy poplars in front of the house, and a large rock maple at the corner of the barn-yard, which the children always tapped in the spring to get sap to drink and make sap coffee. There was a real hospitable look about the old homestead; it seemed to say, "There's pork in the cellar, there's corn in the crib, hay in the barn, and a good fire on the hearth: walk in, neighbor, and make yourself at home."

But the popularity of Captain Rhines among his neighbors had a deeper root than this. A great many of the young men in the neighborhood had been their first voyage to sea with him; he had treated them in such a manner, had taken so much pains to advance them in their profession, that they respected and loved him ever after.

When it was known in the neighborhood that Captain Rhines was going to sea, the question was not, how he should *get* men, but how he should get *rid* of them, there were so many eager for the berth.

It would have done your heart good to have seen the happy faces of the men grouped together on that ship's forecastle, waiting, like hounds straining in the leash, for the order to man the windlass; not an old broken-down shellback among them, but all the neighbors' boys, in their red shirts, and duck trousers white as the driven snow, which their mothers had washed.

As each one of them had a character to sustain, was anxious to outdo his shipmate, and the greater portion of them were in love with some neighbor's daughter, and expected to be married as soon as they were master of a ship, it is evident there was very little to do in the way of discipline. It was a jolly

13

sight, when there came a gale of wind, to see them scamper up the rigging, racing with each other for the "weather-earing."

Captain Rhines, though a large and powerfully built man, was a pygmy to his son Ben. Ben measured, crooks and all, six feet two inches in height, weighing two hundred and thirty pounds. He was possessed of strength in proportion to his size, and, what was more remarkable, was as spry as an eel, and could jump out of a hogshead without touching his hands to it. His neighbors called him "Lion Ben." He obtained the appellation from this circumstance.

One day when the inhabitants of the district were at work on the roads, they dug out a large rock. Ben, then nineteen years of age, took it up, carried it out of the road, dropped it, and said it might stay there till they raised another man in town strong enough to take it back.

He was now twenty-six years of age, of excellent capacity, and good education for the times, his father having sent him to Massachusetts to school. It was very difficult to provoke him; but when, after long provocation, he became enraged, his temper broke out in an instant, and he knew no measure in his wrath. His townsmen loved him, because he used his strength to protect the weak, and were at the same time excessively proud of him, as in all the neighboring towns there was not a man that could throw him, or that even dared to take hold of him.

He had a large chair made on purpose for him to sit in, and tools for him to work with; and if anybody lent a crowbar to Captain Rhines, they always said, "Don't let Ben use it," as in that case it was sure to come home bent double, and had to be sent to the blacksmith's to be straightened.

He was passionately fond of gunning, and would risk life and limb to shoot a goose or sea-duck. Though he had followed the sea since he was seventeen years of age, yet he was greatly attached to the soil, and when at home loved to work on it. It was a curious sight to see this great giant weeding the garden, or at work upon his sister's flower-bed.

He was a generous-hearted creature; when anybody was sick or poor he would get all the young folks together, make a bee, get in their corn, do their planting, or cut their winter's wood for them. He had often done this for the widow Hadlock, who was their nearest neighbor. The widow Hadlock's husband, a very enterprising sea captain, had died at sea, in the prime of life, leaving his widow with a young family, a farm, a fine house well furnished, but nothing more. The broken-hearted woman had struggled very hard to keep the homestead for her children, and the whole family together. Being a woman of great prudence, industry, and judgment, with the help of good neighbors, she had succeeded. Her oldest son was now able to manage the farm, and the bitterness of the struggle was past.

The tax-gatherer came to the widow for the taxes.

"Why, Mr. Jones," said the widow, "you tax me altogether too much; I have not so much property."

"O, Mrs. Hadlock," said he, "we tax you for your faculty."

Notwithstanding all the sterling qualities we have enumerated, the personal appearance of Ben Rhines was anything but an exponent of his character. There was such an enormous enlargement of the muscles of the shoulders, and his neck was so short, that his head seemed to come out of the middle of his breast. The great length of his arms was exaggerated by the stoop in his shoulders: though his legs and hips were large, yet the tremendous development of the upper part of the body gave him the appearance of being top-heavy.

From such a square-jawed fellow you would naturally expect to proceed a deep bass voice; but from this monstrous bulk came a soft, child-like voice, such as we sometimes hear from very fat people; and unless he was greatly excited, the words were slowly drawled: the entire impression made by him upon a stranger was that of a great, listless, inoffensive man, without penetration to perceive, or courage to resist, imposition.

But never was the proverb, "Appearances are deceitful," more strikingly verified than in this instance. That listless exterior, and almost infantile voice, concealed a mind clear and well informed, and a temper, that when goaded beyond the limits of forbearance, broke out like the eruption of a volcano.

In his position as mate of a vessel it became his duty to control men of all nations. Being well aware that his appearance was calculated to invite aggression, he took singular methods to escape it. He knew that his temper, when it reached a certain point, was beyond his control. He also knew his strength; and as the good-natured giant didn't want to hurt anybody when milder methods would answer the purpose, he would come along just as the ship was getting under way, the men at the topsail halyards, and reaching up above all the rest, bring them down in a heap on deck, causing those that were singing to bite their tongues. Sometimes when two or three sailors were heaving with the handspikes to roll up a spar to the ringbolts, singing out and making a great fuss, he would seize hold of the end of it, and heave it into its bed apparently without any effort, while the men would wink to each other and reflect upon the consequences of having a brush with such a mate as that.

By proceeding in this way, though he had taken up one or two that had

15

insulted him beyond endurance, and smashed them down upon the ground, kicked a truckman into the dock who was beating his horse with a cordwood stick, he never struck but one man in his life, which happened in this wise.

Ben was on board a ship in port, with only a cook and two boys, the captain having gone home, and the rest of the crew being discharged. He hired an English sailor to help the boys trim some ballast in the hold; they complained that he kicked and abused them.

Ben told them to go to work again, and he would see about it. After dinner he lay down in his berth for a nap, when he was disturbed by a terrible outcry in the hold, and, going down, found the sailor beating the boys with a rope's end. He asked him what he was doing that for; the man said they wouldn't work, and were saucy to him. Ben replied that the boys were good boys, that he had always known them, and that he mustn't strike the boys. The bully asked him if he meant to take it up. Ben replied that he didn't wish to take it up, but he mustn't strike the boys.

The sailor then threatened to strike him; upon which Ben stood up before him, and folding his arms on his breast, in his drawling, childish way, told him to strike. The man struck, when Ben inflicted upon him such a terrible blow, that, falling upon the ballast, he lay and quivered like an ox when he is struck down by the butcher.

"O, Mr. Rhines," exclaimed the terrified boys, "you've killed him, you've killed him!"

"Well," he replied in his quiet way, "if I've killed him, I've laid him out."

CHAPTER III.

TIGE RHINES.

There was another member of the family whose qualities deserve especial mention—the great Newfoundland dog.

We have already alluded to the captain's fondness for the race: there was always a dog in his father's family. Often had old Lion furnished them with a meal, or detected the ambush of the lurking Indian. As though to round and complete the sum of kindly associations clustering around this pleasant household, even Tiger partook of the good qualities of the family. Captain Rhines said that he wouldn't have a dog that would make the neighbors dislike to come to the house; but as for Tiger, he was both a gentleman and a Christian.

The breed of dogs to which he belonged are both by nature and inclination fitted for the water, and as insensible to the cold as a white bear. Their skin is greasy; there is a fine wool under their long hair which turns water; when they come ashore they give themselves a shake or two and are nearly dry. They are also partially web-footed; they do not swim like common dogs, thrusting their paws out before them like a hog, but spread out their great feet and strike out sidewise like a boy.

The way in which the captain made the acquaintance of Tige was on this wise: One of his last voyages was to Trieste; he met in the street a fine-looking dog carrying a basket full of eggs; greatly pleased with the appearance of the animal, he turned to look after him, when, as he passed a stable door, a dog as large as himself attacked him in the rear. He bore it patiently till he came to a house, when, putting down his eggs, he turned upon his persecutor, and gave him such a mauling that he was glad to escape on three legs, and covered with blood. The captain followed the dog to a menagerie, where he ascertained that it was the dog's daily duty to bring eggs to feed the monkeys; that he had flogged the other a day or two before, who thought to avenge himself by attacking him at a disadvantage.

The captain succeeded in buying the animal, though he never dared to tell what he gave for him.

"Were I not pushed for money," said the showman, after the bargain was concluded, "I never would have parted with him; he will protect your person and your property; you never will be sorry that you bought him, though I shall often regret that I was obliged to sell him."

Captain Rhines soon found that the showman had spoken the truth. He could leave the most valuable articles on the wharf, and trust them to his keeping.

So well was his disposition known, that not a child in the neighborhood feared to come to the house by night or day. He would permit any person to inspect the premises, but not to touch the least thing.

They might, in the night time, knock at the door as long as they pleased; but if they put their hand on the latch, he would knock it off with his paw, and show his teeth in a way that discouraged further attempts. When the little children came who could not knock loud enough to be heard, he would bark for them till he brought somebody to the door.

There was nothing so attractive to Tige as a baby on the floor, nor anything in which he so much delighted as to follow them around, and with his great tongue lick meat and gingerbread out of their fists. No wonder his master said he was a gentleman and a Christian; for though he would tear a thief in a moment, these little tots would get on him as he lay in the grass, stuff his mouth and nose full of clover heads to hear him sneeze, and, when tired of that, lie down on him and go to sleep.

Next to playing with babies, his favorite employment was fishing. In a calm day, when the water was clear, he would swim off to a dry ledge, called Seal Rock, in the cove before the house, dive down, and bring up a fish every time.

The fish always worked off on the ebb tide, and came up on the flood. Tige knew as well when it was flood tide, and time to go floundering, as did John Rhines, his bosom friend and constant companion. Tige always went to meeting, and slept *on* the horse-block in fair weather, and *under* it in foul.

The good women said, they did wish Tige Rhines would stay at home, for when they had fixed the children all up nice to go to meeting, they were sure to be hugging him, and he would slobber them all over, lick their hair down about their eyes, and chew their bonnet "ribbins" into strings.

Captain Rhines hired Sam Hadlock to help him hoe. When he went home Saturday night, he hung up his hoe in the shed, as he expected to work there the next week, but, finding his mother's corn was suffering to be hoed, went back to get it. The family had gone to bed, and Tige wouldn't let him touch it, though they were great friends, and he was the next neighbor. He was going into the house without knocking, for they didn't fasten doors in those days;

but the instant he put his hand on the latch, the dog knocked it off with his paw, and he was obliged to knock till Ben came and got the hoe for him.

A more singular proof of his sagacity occurred soon after. They had a fuss in the district with the schoolmaster, and a lawsuit grew out of it. Captain Rhines's daughter was summoned as a witness by the master. He came one evening to see her about it, when the rest of the family were from home. Tiger thought, as she was alone, all was not right; so he waits upon the master to the door, and when she opened it, stood up on his hind legs, and put his fore paws on the master's shoulders, and without offering to harm him, kept him there. They had to do their talking over Tiger's shoulder; but when it was finished, he made no objection to his departure.

In the cove before the house was a beach of fine white sand, without a stone in it, which when wet was as hard as a floor. The children were never tired of playing on this spot. The upper portion, which was only occasionally wet by the tide, was dry and the sand loose, while the lower part, which the water had recently left, was hard and smooth to run on, thus affording them a variety of amusements. Some would run races on the beach, chase the retreating waves, and then scamper back, screaming with delight, as the wave broke around their heels.

Others sailed boats, waded in the water after shells, and if they could get Tige, they would spit on a stick and fling it as far as they could into the water, and send him in to fetch it out, while those who were learning to swim would catch hold of his tail and be towed ashore. While all this was going on at the water's edge, another party on the upper portion would be rolling over on the hot, clean sand, and building forts, and digging wells with clam shells; others still, under the clay bank, were making mud puddings and pies, and roasting clams at a great fire made of drift-wood.

Parents did not like very well to have the children, especially the little ones, play there so much, for fear of their getting drowned; and the larger ones could not well be spared from work to go with them; but they could not find it in their hearts to forbid them, they had such a good time of it. So, once or twice every week during the summer, a group of little folks would come to the captain's, and one of them, making her best "courtesy," would say,—

"Captain Rhines, me, and Eliza Ann Hadlock, and Caroline Griffin, and the Warren girls, are going down to the cove to play, and my marm wants to know if Tige can go and take care of us."

Tige, who knew what the children wanted as well as they did themselves, would stand looking his master in the face, wagging his tail, and saying, as plain as a dog could say, "Do let me go, sir."

Captain Rhines, one afternoon, set a herring net in the mouth of the cove. These nets are very long, and are set by fastening the upper edge to a rope, called the *cork-rope*. On this rope are strung corks, or wooden buoys made of cedar, which keep it on top of the water. It is then stretched out, and the two ends fastened to the bottom by "grapplings." To each end larger buoys are fastened; weights are then attached to the lower edge, so that it hangs perpendicular in the water. The fish run against it in the dark, and are caught by their gills.

It is the nature of Newfoundland dogs to bring ashore whatever they see floating. Tige went down to the Seal Rock floundering, and saw the buoys bobbing up and down in the water; away he swims to bring them ashore. Finding them fast to the bottom, what does he do, but with his sharp teeth gnaws off the cork-rope and set them adrift? till there were not enough left to float the net, and it sank to the bottom. He then carried all the floats to the Seal Rock and piled them up, and thinking he had done a meritorious act, lay down to rest himself after his labors.

The next morning Captain Rhines and Ben went to take up their net. They thought some vessel must either have run over it and carried it off on her keel or rudder, or else that so many fish were meshed as to sink it. They grappled and brought it up, when, to their astonishment, there was not a fish in it, the cork-rope cut to pieces, the two large buoys and about two thirds of the net-buoys gone.

But as they pulled home by the Seal Rock there was every one of the missing floats, with the marks of Tiger's teeth in the soft wood. Captain Rhines was in a towering passion, because it was not only a great deal of work to grapple for the net, but the cork-rope, which was valuable in those days, was all cut to pieces.

He sent John up to the house after Tige, and got a big stick to beat him. The beach was covered with children of all ages. They left their sports and ran to the spot. John Rhines begged his father not to lick the dog, while the children began to cry; but the captain was determined. "Father," said Ben, "I wouldn't beat him; if you beat him for bringing these floats ashore, he won't go after birds when you shoot them." Upon this, the captain, who was an inveterate gunner, flung away the stick; and the children, drying up their tears, took Tige off to frolic with them.

The miller's daughter, three years and a half old, had a speckled kitten; a brutal boy drowned it in the mill-pond. The little creature went down to look for her kitten, and fell in. Just then Captain Rhines and Tige came to the mill with a grist. The child had gone down for the third time. He jumped from the horse, and threw in a stone where he saw the bubbles come up. Tige instantly followed the stone, and brought up the child with just the breath of life in it.

The overjoyed mother hugged the child, and then hugged Tige. The miller gave him a brass collar, with an account of this brave act engraved upon it.

Ever after this he had a warm place in the affections of the whole community, and was almost as much beloved and respected as his master.

The sentiments of the young folks, in respect to Tige, were put to the test the next summer. A boy came there in a fishing vessel, who was full of pranks, had never received any culture, knew nothing of the history of Tige, and perhaps, if he had, would not have cared; to gratify a malicious disposition, he put some spirits of turpentine on him, causing him great agony. The enraged children enticed the boy to the beach, and while he was in swimming, carried off his clothes, and, having prepared themselves with sticks, fell upon him as he came out of the water, and beat him to a jelly.

A few days after the event just narrated, Captain Rhines was sitting in the door after dinner, when he saw little Fannie Williams, the miller's daughter, coming into the yard. She was evidently bent on business of importance, for, though passionately fond of flowers, she never looked at the lilies, hollyhocks, and morning glories, on each side of her, but walking directly up to him, and putting both hands on his knees, said, with the tears glistening in her little eyes, "You won't whip Tige, will you, if he does do naughty things?"

"God bless the child!" said the captain, taking her in his lap and kissing her, "have you come way down here to ask me that?"

"Nobody knowed it, and nobody told me to come; I comed my own self, 'cause he shan't be whipped. Fannie loves Tige."

"You've good reason to love him, for if it had not been for him you'd been a dead baby now. I never will whip him, nor let anybody else."

The captain then took her by the hand, and led her into the orchard, where he picked up some pears, and put in a basket; he then culled a bunch of flowers as large as she could carry, and putting the handle of the basket in Tige's mouth, sent him home with her. The little girl, with her fears quieted, trudged along, putting her flowers to Tige's nose for him to smell of, telling him he shouldn't be licked, 'cause Captain Rhines said so.

CHAPTER IV.

BEN'S COURTSHIP.

BEN had never been to sea with his father. Captain Rhines didn't believe it was a good plan for relations to be shipmates; he didn't want his son to be "ship's cousin," but to rise on his own merits, as his father had done before him; and if he couldn't do that, then he might stay down. But Ben had proved himself to be a man of capacity. The owners were all willing, and his father wanted him to take the ship and let him stay at home.

Ben gladly accepted the offer, and was making preparations to go; but there was a matter of great importance for him to settle, before he left home. Ben loved Sally Hadlock, though he had never dared to tell her of it.

She had a great many admirers among the young men, and he felt that it was risking altogether too much to go on a long voyage, and run the venture of Sally's being snapped up by some of them before his return. The greatest source of apprehension in his mind was the fact, that he heard she had said, she never could, nor would, marry a man that followed the sea.

Her father and oldest brother were lost at sea. Sally could never forget the agony of her mother when her father's sea chest came home, nor the trial of those bitter years, during which she and her mother had struggled along, and kept the family together until the younger children grew up.

Sally Hadlock was a poor girl, but she was as pretty as a May morning. Though she knew scarcely a note of music, she could warble like a bird, and, as the neighbors said, "she was faculized." Everybody loved and respected Sally for her kindness to her mother, and because she was as modest as she was beautiful, and as lively as a humming-bird. Her mother idolized her, as well she might.

Never was the widow so happy as when, over a good cup of souchong, she descanted upon the fine qualities of her daughter, utterly regardless of Sally's blushes, and whispered, "O, don't, mother." "Yes," the old lady would say, shoving her spectacles up on her cap, and stirring slowly her tea, "I'll put my Sally, though I say it that shouldn't say it, for taking a fleece of wool as it comes from the sheep's back, and making it into cloth, against any girl in the town; and then she always has such good luck making soap, and such luck with her bread! she beats me out and out in hot biscuit. You see this tablecloth; well, she spun the flax, and bleached the thread, drew it into the loom, and wove it, all sole alone."

Sally was not without some dim perception of Ben's attachment to her. She knew that he was very fond of her brother Sam; and that if he wanted to borrow anything they had, he would always come himself, both to get it and to bring it home.

When he came home from sea, he always brought presents for the widow Hadlock. Many of them, though very beautiful, didn't seem altogether adapted to an old widow; and then her mother would say, "Sally, these things are very beautiful, but I shall never put off my mourning for your dear father; they would be very becoming to you."

Ben went to singing-school, in the school-house. A young man had recently come into the village from Salem, as a singing-master. He had a way that took mightily with the girls. This excited a general antipathy to him among all the young men in the place, who, since his advent, found themselves at a discount with the ladies. Latterly, his attentions had been directed particularly to Sally Hadlock, as the prettiest girl in the village.

The house being crowded one evening, Ben had gone into the seat usually reserved for the singers. The singing-master, who was an empty coxcomb, with nothing but good looks to recommend him, ordered him out. Ben, with his usual good nature, would have obeyed; but the tone was so contemptuous, and the place so public (probably Sally's presence might have had something to do with it), that it stung; Ben replied that he sat very well, and remained as he was.

This drew the eyes of all upon him, as expecting something interesting. In a few moments his tormentor returned, and assured him, if he did not move, and that quick, he would be put out. Upon this, Ben rose up to his full height, and looking down upon the frightened man of music, said, "I don't think there are men enough in this school-house to put me out."

This sally was received with a universal shout by the audience, who not only had not the least doubt of the fact, but also rejoiced in the discomfiture of the puppy.

Sally was very much grieved at the master's insulting treatment of Ben, who had done so much for her mother. It is said that all women are hero-worshippers.

When she saw him so completely frightened out of his impertinence, and made ridiculous, noticed the forbearance of Ben, who might have squat him up like a fly between his fingers and thumb, she became conscious of a tenderer feeling for her old schoolmate, who that night went home with her and her mother for the first time.

Ben now determined to make a bold push, and go and see Sally Sunday night, though he knew she, and everybody else, would know what it meant. It seems very singular that Ben Rhines, who had been half over the world, and in a privateer, should be afraid to go over to the widow Hadlock's before dark; but he was: so he broke the matter to his most intimate friend, Sam Johnson, who offered to go with him the next Sunday night.

It was a pleasant Sabbath afternoon, in August, about four o'clock. Captain Rhines had been sitting in his arm-chair reading the Apocrypha, and fell asleep.

Ben was sitting at the window, all dressed up, quite nervous, waiting for Sam.

Sam came at length, and asked Ben if he wanted to go into the pastures and get a few blueberries. Ben assented, when, to their astonishment, old Captain Rhines roused up and inquired, "Where are you going, boys?"

"We're just going out to get a few blueberries."

"Well, I don't care if I go, too."

Here was a dilemma; but love helps wit. They found a thick bush for the old gentleman to pick, crawled away on their hands and knees to a safe distance, then got on their feet, and ran for the widow Hadlock's.

The old captain having hallooed for them long after they were in the widow's parlor, finally went home. Just as they expected, they were asked to stop to supper.

After supper, Sally and her mother went out to milking, while Ben and Sam leaned on the fence to look at them. The old speckled cow, which Sally had milked ever since she was a girl, acted as if bewitched: she switched Sally's comb out of her head with her tail, and finally put her foot in the milk-pail.

While all this was going on, Sam Johnson unaccountably disappeared. Ben could do no less than offer to carry in the milk for them; was invited to spend the evening; and the old lady, excusing herself on account of ill health, slipped off to bed, and Ben and Sally were left together.

In due time Ben asked Sally if she liked him well enough to marry him.

Now Sally was a good, sensible New England girl: she didn't faint nor scream, but she blushed a little, and finally consented to marry him, on condition that he should give up going to sea, and stay at home with her.

24

The reader must bear in mind that this is not a love scene of a sensation novel, but conversation of people, who, loving each other sincerely, looked upon married life as a sacred obligation, in which they put their whole heart, and expected to find their sole happiness.

Ben did not therefore reply that he loved Sally to distraction, that he could not exist a moment without her, and that he would never dream of going to sea again; but, after some considerable hesitation, he at length moved his chair nearer to Sally, and looking up full in her face, said, "Sally, you and I have known each other.from the time we made bulrush caps together in your mother's pasture, when we were children, till now; and I think you know me well enough to know that I am a man of few words, and would never ask a woman to marry me unless I really loved her, and intended to support her, for you know that must be thought of.

"As for going to sea, though I have been fortunate, and risen in my profession faster than any young man in town, faster, perhaps, than I ought,— for I was mate of a ship before I was twenty,—though I have no reason to be afraid of men, and can handle the roughest of them like children, and care nothing for hardship, yet I never liked the sea. O, how I have longed, on some East India voyage, to see an acre of green grass, or hear a robin sing! I don't like to feel that people obey me just because they are afraid of me, and to go stalking round the decks like some of those giants we read of in the old story books. I do love the land better than the sea. I love the flowers; I love to plough and hoe; I love to see things grow. I'm as loath to go to sea as you can be to have me;" and he put his arm around her neck and kissed her; "but the seaman's life is my profession. I have spent many of the best years of my life, employed the time that might have been devoted to learning a trade, or some other business on shore, in fitting myself for it. I now have a ship offered me: this affords me at once the opportunity of reaping the fruits of my past labor, and supporting a wife; besides, Sally, we are both poor. You may think it strange, that, as I have been officer of a vessel for some time, I should not have laid up something; but my father became involved some years ago, and I felt it my duty to help him out; and I am neither sorry for it nor ashamed of it. This was the reason I did not dress better, because I felt that I ought to economize, for the sake of the best parents ever a boy had. I suppose many people, who knew I was earning a good deal of money, thought I was mean, or spent it in some bad way; and perhaps you did."

"No, Ben," replied Sally; "I knew better than that. I knew that, if you didn't, like a snail, put everything on your back, you were always ready to help any one who needed it; and no person can go on long in a bad course without those who love them finding it out."

"You see how it is, Sally, if I take this ship, I am at once in circumstances to be married, with the prospect of a comfortable living. To be sure, I could work on the land, for I was a farmer till I was seventeen; but then I should have to run in debt to buy it. There is not much money to be got off a farm; it always took about what father earned to pay the hired help, the taxes, and family expenses, and he soon had to go to sea again for more."

Poor Sally listened, as Ben thus placed before her the "inevitable logic of facts."

She looked first this way, and then that, and finally laid her head on Ben's shoulder, and cried like a child.

Ben was greatly distressed: he knew not what to say, and remained for a long time silent; at length he said, "There is a way that I have thought of, but I didn't like to mention it, for fear—" Here he hesitated.

"For fear of what?" cried Sally, lifting her head from his shoulder, and looking at him through her tears.

"Why, for fear, if I should do it, and you should marry me on the strength of it, and we should be poor, see hard times, and people should look down on us, that then you might perhaps feel—" And here he stopped again.

"Feel what?"

"Why," stammered Ben, finding he must out with it, "feel that if you had only married some of these young men that I know have offered themselves to you, and that had rich fathers, instead of poor Ben Rhines, you wouldn't have needed to have brought the water to wash your hands."

"When I marry," replied Sally, bluntly, "I shall not marry anybody's father, but the boy I love. Now, let's hear your plan, Ben."

"You know," he replied, more slowly than he had ever spoken before in his whole life, "the island off in the bay that father has had the care of so many years?"

"What, Elm Island?"

"That's it."

"Yes, indeed! I've been there a hundred times with our Sam and Seth Warren, after berries."

"It's the best land that ever lay out doors, covered with a heavy growth of spruce and pine, fit for spars; many of them would run seventy feet without a limb. I think old Mr. Welch would sell it on credit to any one he knew, and that anybody might cut off the timber, and have the land, and wood enough to

26

burn, left clear. It would make a splendid farm, and a man might pick up considerable money by gunning and fishing; but," said Ben, his countenance falling, "what a place for a woman! No society, no neighbors, right among the breakers; and sometimes, in the winter, there'll be a month nobody can get on nor off. It would be a good place to get a living, and lay up money; but no woman would go on there, and a man would be a brute to ask her. I'm sorry I said anything about it."

"There's one woman will go on there," replied Sally, "and not repent of it after she gets there either; and that woman's Sally Hadlock. I hold that if a girl loves a man well enough to marry him, she'll be contented where he is, and she won't be contented where he isn't. As to the society, I had rather be alone with my husband than have all the society in the world without him. I had rather be on an island with my husband, working hard, and carrying my share of the load, than to be in the best society, and have every comfort, and at the same time know that my husband is beating about at sea, in sickly climates, perhaps dying, with nobody to do for him, in order to support me in luxury and laziness, or in circumstances of comfort which he cannot enjoy with me; and I say that any woman, that *is* a woman, will say amen to it. We may have a hard scratch of it at first, and have to live rough; but I have always been poor; it's nothing new to me. What reason on earth is there, bating sickness or death, why we should not get along? I've always maintained myself, and helped maintain my mother and family. You have maintained yourself, paid your father's debts, and more too, for you have helped my mother lots."

"Yes, but I was going to sea then," put in Ben.

"It is strange, then," continued Sally, without heeding the interruption, "that we two, who have supported ourselves and other folks, can't support our own selves. I see how it is, Ben; this island can be bought very cheap, on account of the disadvantages of living on it; that you can pay for it by your own labor, and see no other way of getting your living on the land. Is that it, Ben?"

"That is it."

"Well, then," replied this noble New England girl, reddening to the very roots of her hair, and her eyes flashing through her tears, "I will marry you, and go to that island with you; we will take the bitter with the sweet; we will suffer and enjoy together. If you love me well enough to give up a ship, and go on to that island to live with me, I love you well enough to go on it and be happy with you. I thank God, that if he has given me a handsome face, as they say, he has not given me an empty head nor an idle hand to go with it. I have worked, and saved, and denied myself for my mother and brothers, and have been right happy and well thought of in doing it. I can do the same for my husband; and if any think *less* of me on that account, I shan't have them for next door neighbors to twit me of it. My home is in my husband's heart, and where his interest and duty lie."

Ben thought she never looked half so beautiful before, and imprinted a fervent kiss upon the lips that had uttered such noble sentiments. The day was breaking as they separated.

CHAPTER V.

SALLY TELLS HER MOTHER ALL ABOUT IT.

SALLY slept in the same room with her mother. The old lady waked, and finding Sally's bed not tumbled, called loudly for her daughter. When she came, her mother said, "Why, Sally, your bed has not been tumbled this live-long night; how flushed you look! your hair is all of a frizzle, and you've been crying: what is the matter with you?"

Poor Sally, nervous and excited after the night's conflict, made a clean breast of it.

"Mother, I've said I'd have Ben, that is, if you are willing," and, burying her face in the pillow, she burst into a flood of tears. The good old lady was not so much troubled by tears as Ben had been, but, putting her arms round her daughter, said, "That's right, dear; cry as much as you please; it'll ease your mind, and do you good;" and, wrapped up in her own reflections about an event she had long foreseen, patiently waited till Sally should think best to speak. Finding Sally not inclined to break the silence, she said, "I think you could not have done better than to be engaged to Ben; and I'm sure you could not have done anything so pleasing to me; that is, if you love him, for that is the main thing.

"I've always told you it is very wrong for a girl to marry a man whom she doesn't love; it isn't right in the sight of God, and always leads to misery. Ben isn't so good-looking as some young men, nor rich in this world's goods; but he has good learning and good manners: he is of a good family; can do more work than any three young men in town; and for all he is such a giant, never gives a misbeholden word to any one. You've known him from childhood. It's a great deal better to marry him with only the clothes to his back, and the good principles that are in him, than to marry some one who is rich and handsome now, may die a drunkard, and perhaps, some time, throw up to your poverty."

"O, I know all that, mother; but there's something else, which, perhaps, I ought not to have done without asking you. I've promised to go and live on Elm Island, right in the woods, and among the breakers;" and then she told her mother every word that she and Ben had said, from beginning to end, throwing in, as a sweetener, a circumstance which she knew would have great influence with her parent; "but then, you know, he has promised never to go

29

to sea any more."

She was most agreeably disappointed when the widow, after a little pause, replied in her mild way, "I not only approve of what you've done, but should have been very sorry if you had done otherwise. Your grandmother, girl, was born in old Rowley, Massachusetts, was brought up to have everything she wanted, and knew nothing of hardships; but she married your grandfather because she loved him, though he was a poor man. They came down here, and took up this farm when it was all woods. I've stood in the door of our old house, and seen eleven wolves come off Birch Point and go on the ice to Oak Island: one of them had lost his leg in a trap, and could not keep up with the rest, and they would squat down on the ice and wait for him. They burnt up their first house in clearing the land, and had to live in a brush camp till they built another. I've heard mother say, a hundred times, that the happiest years of her life were those hard years; that the anticipation of living easier by and by, and having a good farm, was better than the good farm when they got it; that there was nothing in her well-to-do life afterwards to compare with the satisfaction of looking back to those hard times when she had the strength to endure those hardships. Then her face would light up, her eyes kindle, and the color come into her old cheeks; and as I looked at her, I used to hope that I should live to see such pleasant hardships, to be glad of and tell about when I was old.

"Well, Sally, I've had *troubles*, and *bitter* ones; the sea has been a devourer to me; but not *hardships*, because I married and lived at home; but you have the chance, girl, to know something about it. Don't be afraid of being poor; people here don't know what poverty is. Go to Liverpool, if you want to see what real poverty is, as I have been many a time with your poor father, who is dead and gone. A man with a farm is sure of a living, and a good one, too; the farmers feed the world, and they are great fools if they don't lick their own fingers. Two thirds of the merchants fail; a great many seamen die at sea, and it's a dog's life at best. The sailor is only anxious when the wind blows; but the wind blows all the time for the poor wife at home, and her pillow is often wet with tears.

"The last time I was in Rowley, I saw rich men's sons; whose fathers scorned your grandfather because he was a farmer, going about killing hogs and cutting wood for folks. For a farmer to kill his own hogs, or to change work with his neighbors to kill theirs, then they help him kill his, or to cut his own wood, is a very different thing from what it is for people, who felt as large as they did once, and, in their pride and prosperity, looked down on every one that labored, to have to do it for a living. Your grandmother said, it used to make her blood run cold to see them come into the house of God with such an air, getting up and sitting down two or three times, flaunting with their 'ribbins,' and chattering like a striped squirrel on the side of a tree. I was up there the year before Sam was born; and now to see how they live! just the least little scriffin of bread and butter, or a little pie; the least little piece of meat, about as big as your hand, which they run to the butcher's to get, for they never have anything in the cellar; then, instead of doing as we do, cutting it thick, and telling everybody to help themselves, they cut it into little slices and help them, for fear, I suppose, they should take too much; and then so many compliments to so little victuals! But they put it on their backs, Sally; that's what they do with it; they put it on their backs. As they have no hearty victuals and hard work to give them color, they paint their faces, and look out of the windows, as Jezebel did: they spend most all their time looking out of the windows."

Sally rejoiced to find that, when following the inclinations of her own heart, she had done just right; and with a face from which every trace of tears had vanished, replied, "I thought I knew your mind, mother; but I must go and get breakfast, for I thought I heard Sam getting up."

CHAPTER VI.

BEN BUYS ELM ISLAND.

BEN went to Boston to see the old merchant, whom he knew very well, having often seen him at his father's when he was on his summer visits. The good merchant, who had been a poor boy, and earned his property by his own industry, and was both too wise and too good to value himself by his wealth, received Ben so kindly, that he told him all his heart; what he wanted the island for, of the promise he had made to Sally, and all about it. He commended Ben; told him he knew Sally's father (that he had sailed for him), and her mother, too; she was of good blood; there was a great deal in the blood. He told him he would have a happy life; that he had always regretted he had not been a farmer himself. He had worked night and day, amassed a large property, educated his family, and looked forward to the time when they would be a source of happiness to him; but his children were indolent, knew he had wealth, and had no desire to do anything for themselves; he feared they would spend his money faster than he had earned it. "Indeed, Ben," replied the merchant, with a sigh, "I would much rather take your chance for happiness, and a comfortable living in this world, than that of either of my sons."

Ben was utterly amazed. He had thought, when looking upon that splendid furniture, and wealth and taste there displayed, that people in such circumstances must be extremely happy; but, as he was not deficient in shrewdness, he learned a lesson that effectually repressed any desire to murmur at his own lot.

The merchant then said to him, "Mr. Rhines, if you were buying this island on speculation, I should charge you a round price for it, as the timber is valuable, easy of access by water, the taxes are merely nominal, and your father prevents it from being plundered; but as you are buying it to make a home of, and I know what you have done for your father,—for he told me himself,—I shall let you have it at a low rate, and any length of time you wish to pay for it in."

As they parted, he encouraged Ben by telling him that a Down-easter would get rich where anybody else would starve.

It was now the month of October. Ben proposed that they should be married; Sally should live with her mother during the winter, while he went on to the island, cut a freight of spars, dug a cellar before the ground froze, and made preparations for building in the spring. But Sally declared she would as lief have Ben at sea as have him on this island, running back and forth in the cold winter; that after a man had been at work a whole week, he didn't want to pull a boat six miles, and be wet all through with spray; that there would be a great many days, when, if he was off, he could not get on, and if he was on, he could not get off, and there would be a great deal of time lost. Man and wife ought not to be separated; 'twas no way to live; she would go to the island and live with him.

"Live where, Sally?" inquired Ben.

"Why, with you. I suppose you will live somewhere—won't you?"

"Well," replied Ben, with a comical look at his great limbs, "I can live anywhere a Newfoundland dog can; but I shouldn't want you to, nor should I consent to it. I expect to take some hands with me, build a half-faced cabin, good enough for us to live in, cut spars and timber, build a house next summer, and move in the fall."

"It'll cost you a good deal to build this house."

"Why, yes. I can get the frame on the island, and the stuff for the boards and shingles. I shall have to buy bricks, and lime, and nails, and hire a joiner."

"What does't cost to build a log house?"

"Next to nothing, because we can build them of logs that are fit for nothing else."

"Are they warm?"

"Warmest things that ever you saw. The boards on a house are only an inch thick, but you can have the logs three feet thick, if you like."

"Are they tight?"

"They can be made as tight as a cup."

"I don't think, then, a Newfoundland dog would be likely to suffer much in your shanty."

"I was telling how a log house *could* be made. I don't expect to take much pains with mine."

"Would not all this timber that you are going to make frame, boards, and shingles of, fetch a good price in the market?"

"Why, yes, it would nearly all make spars."

"Then you should build, instead of a half-faced cabin, a real log house, 'three feet thick,' if you like, and 'as tight as a cup.' I'll go on with you; it'll be a great deal better than to take turns in cooking, and live like pigs, as men always do when they live together. I've heard you say you had rather eat off a chip, and then throw it away, than eat off a china plate, and have to wash it when you were done; then there would be no time lost. When you came in from your work you would have your meals warm, and we would have a real sociable time in the evening."

"O, that will never do."

"But it will do, Ben; you've just said that a log house was warm and comfortable."

"Indeed it is," chimed in the old lady, who, with her spectacles above her cap, and her hands upon her knees, sat leaning forward, her whole soul in her face, while the favorite cat, who for twenty years had spent the evening in her patron's lap, stood with one paw upon her mistress's knee, and the other uplifted with an air of astonishment at being prevented from securing her accustomed place,—"indeed it is. Mother used to say this house never began to be so warm or so tight as the old log house."

"O, dear, Sally!" exclaimed Ben, greatly troubled; "I thought 'twas bad enough to take you on to the island to live at all, and now you insist on living in a log house. What will folks say? They will say, there's Sally Hadlock, that might have had her pick of the likeliest fellows in town, and never have had to bring the water to wash her hands, has taken up with Ben Rhines, and gone to live in a log shanty on Elm Island."

"Look here, Ben," replied Sally; "suppose my father had been a fisherman, and lived on Elm Island; wouldn't you have come on there and lived with me, though all the young fellows in town had said, There's Ben Rhines, that might have been master of as fine a ship as ever swum, has taken up with old Hadlock's daughter, and gone to live on Elm Island?"

"To be sure I would."

"Well, then," said Sally, coloring, "I hope you don't want me to say, right here before mother, that I'd rather live on Elm Island, in a log house, with the boy I love, than with the best of them in a palace. I want to bring the water to wash my hands. I don't believe that God made us to be idle, or that we are any happier for being so."

"That's right," shouted the old lady, in ecstasies, rising up and kissing her daughter's cheek; "that's the old-fashioned sort of love, that will wear and make happiness, and it's all the thing on this earth that will; it will bear trial; it is a fast color, and won't fade out in washing. Most young people nowadays want to begin where their fathers left off, and they end with running out all that their fathers left them. You're willing to begin and cut your garment according to your cloth, and you will prosper accordingly."

CHAPTER VII.

CAPTAIN RHINES RIDING OUT A GALE BEFORE THE

FIRE.

THE morning succeeding Ben's return from Boston gave tokens of a coming storm.

"Ben," said Captain Rhines, "we're going to have a gale of wind; here's an old roll coming from the east'ard, and the surf is roaring on the White Bull. Let us take the canoe, slip over to Elm Island, and get a couple of lambs, before it comes on. I'm hankering after some fresh 'grub.'"

When, having caught the lamb, they were pulling out of the harbor, the old gentleman, resting on his oar, looked back upon the mass of forest, and said, "What a tremenjus growth here is! here are masts and yards, bowsprits and topmasts, for a ship of the line; and there's no end of the small spars and ranging timber; a great deal of it, too, ought to be cut, for it has got its growth, and will soon be falling down. It is first-rate land, and would make a capital farm after it's cleared. I wish old father Welch had to give it to me; he never would miss it. I believe my soul all he keeps it for is for the sake of coming down here once in three or four years, and going over there gunning 'long with me."

At noon the gale came on with great violence. The captain took advantage of the stormy afternoon to kill a lamb, and have a regular "tuck out" on a sea-pie. Under his directions, Mrs. Rhines lined the large pot with a thick crust, put in the lamb and slices of pork, with flour, water, and plenty of seasoning, and covered the whole with a crust, which Captain Rhines pricked full of holes with his marline-spike.

In addition to this were pudding, pies, and fried apples; coffee, which was seldom indulged in at that day; and last, but not least, a decanter of Holland gin beside his plate. When they had despatched this substantial repast, the family, eight in number, all drew up around the fire. The old house shook with the violence of the gale; the rain came down in torrents; the roar of the surf was distinctly heard in the intervals of the gusts, while the blaze went up the great chimney in sheets of flame.

The old seaman flung off his coat, kicked off his boots, and sitting down in the midst of this happy circle, while the cheerful light flickered around his weather-beaten form, animated by as noble a heart as ever throbbed in human breast, cried, as he listened to the clatter without, "Blow away, my hearty; while she cracks she holds; let them that's got the watch on deck keep it; it's my watch below; eight hours in to-night."

He then sat some time in silence, with his hands clasped over his knees, and looking into a great bed of rock-maple coals. Rousing up at length, he laid his hard hand on his wife's shoulder, and, with an expression of heartfelt happiness on his rugged features, that was perfectly contagious, said, "Mary, I do believe I've never had one hardship too many. When I think how poor I began life; what my parents suffered before they got the land cleared; why, I've seen my poor father hoe corn when he was so weak from hunger that he could scarcely stand. There were times when we should have starved to death, if it had not been for the old dog (stooping down and patting Tige's head, who lay stretched out before the fire, with his nose on his master's foot). How glad I felt as I carried them the first dollar I ever earned! and how glad they were to get it! Well, as I was saying, when I hear the wind whistle, and the sea roar, as it does now, I can't help thinking how many such nights on ship's deck, wet, worn out, listening to the roar of the surf, and expecting the anchors to come home every minute; next 'vige' perhaps in the West Indies; men dying all around me, like sheep, with the yellow fever and black vomit. When I look back, and feel it's all over, that I've got enough to carry me through, can do what little duty I'm fit for, among my comforts, and surrounded by my family, I don't believe I ever could have had the feelings I've got in my bosom to-night, before this comfortable fire, if I hadn't been through the cold, the hunger, the dangers, and all the other miseries first;" and he rolled up his sleeves in the very wantonness of enjoyment, to feel the grateful warmth of fire on his bare flesh.

"I don't wonder you do feel so, husband," replied his wife; "as you say, you've enough to carry you through, as far as this life is concerned; but there is another life after this, and, perhaps, if we get to the better world, that also will seem sweeter for all the crosses we take up, and the self-denial we go through in getting there. I've often told you, Benjamin, that you lack but one thing; for surely never woman had a kinder husband, or children a better father, than you have always been."

"God bless you, Mary!" exclaimed the old seaman in the fulness of his heart; "I've never been half so good a husband as I ought, and must often have hurt your feelings; for I'm a rough old sea-dog; never had any bringing up, but grew up just like the cattle.

"I never see John Strout but it puts me in mind of his oldest brother,

George. We both of us shipped for the first time, as able seamen, in the same vessel; we were about of an age—'townies;' both in the same watch, full of blue veins and vitriol, and were forever trying titles to see which was the best man. It was hard work to tell, when the watch was called, whose feet struck the floor first, his'n or mine. If he got into the rigging before I did, I'd go up hand over fist on the back-stay. I've known him to go on the topsail yard in his shirt-flaps to get ahead of me. We allers made it a p'int to take the weather earing, or the bunt of a sail, away from the second mate, who was the owner's nephew, and put over the head of his betters."

"Was that the reason, father," said Ben, "you wouldn't let me go to sea with you?"

"Yes," he replied. "I've seen enough of these half-and-half fellers put in to command before they are fit for it, just to lose better men's lives, and destroy other people's property."

"I think you have the right of it, father. I don't believe I shall ever be sorry that I came in at the hawsehole, instead of the cabin windows."

"One terrible dark night, in the Gulf," continued the old man, "all hands were on the yard trying to furl the fore-topsail; my sheath-knife was jammed between my body and the yard, so that I couldn't get at it; I reached and took his'n out of the sheath, which he wore behind, and used it; but when I went to put it back again, he was gone; when or how he went, nobody ever knew. I was young then, and new at such things. We had allers been together. I couldn't keep it out of my mind, and didn't want to stay in the vessel after that, for everything I took hold of made me think of him."

"Don't you think, husband," said his wife, "that we ought to think where our blessings come from, and not to think it's all our own work?"

Though Captain Rhines had a rugged temper of his own when roused, with only the education he had picked up at sea, and the culture acquired by friction as he was knocked about in the world, yet he was perfectly moral, and temperate for that day; that is, he was never intoxicated. He had a great respect for religion, especially his wife's, she being a woman of admirable judgment and ardent piety. She was not in the practice of reproving every unguarded expression, and annoying him with exhortations; telling the ministers her anxieties and fears about him, and urging them to talk to him on the spot, whether they were in a frame to converse, or he to listen. She was satisfied he knew where her heart was, that she prayed earnestly for him, and let it rest at that, save when, as on the present occasion, he put the words in her mouth.

"Well, wife," he replied, willing to change the subject, "you've got religion enough for both of us."

"No, husband, that must be every one's own work."

"That ain't all, neither. How many years was I going to sea, just coming home to look in to the door, and say, 'How are you all?' then off again, leaving you to manage farm, family, and hired help! Why, I had scarcely any more care of my family than an ostrich has of her eggs. It seems so much more happy to be with them now, on that very account! I'm half a mind to believe what I then thought to be the worst trial of all, was a blessing, too. I only wish that great critter over there in the corner," pointing to Ben, "could get half so good or good-looking a wife as his mother is; but he's so homely, and there's so much of it, I'm afraid there's not a ghost of a chance for him."

At this there was a general titter amongst the young folks. Ben could hold in no longer, but astonished his parents by telling them what he *had* done, and what he *meant* to do.

"By heavens, Ben!" exclaimed his father, springing to his feet, "you've been fishing to some purpose; I'd moor head and stern to that girl, and lie by her as long as cables and anchor would hold."

"I don't know how to build a log house," said Ben; "and they've been out of use so long round here, I don't know anybody that does."

"I do. Isaac Murch; he helped tear down our old log house, when I was a boy. I suppose you know he is the most ing'nious critter that ever lived. I believe he could make a man, if he should set out for it; and I don't know but he could put a soul in him after he was done. Your grandfather was old and childish, and hated to have the house torn down; so I got Isaac to make a model of it, to please him. I know that he could make one exactly like it, if he had a mind to. I really think I should come to see you a good deal oftener if you were living in the old house, or one that looked just like it."

"But, father, he wouldn't work out."

"He'd do most anything to accommodate you or Sally Hadlock; for, when her father was living, he and Isaac were like two fingers on one hand. I believe he thinks as much of the Hadlock children as he does of his own. There's no knowing how much he's done for those children first and last."

The next day Ben rode over to Isaac's, who, with his wife, gave him a warm welcome.

"By the way," said she, "are you engaged to be married to Sally Hadlock? At any rate, I heard so, and it come pretty straight; own up like a man; murder will out."

"If it is so, I hope it's nothing to be ashamed of."

"Ben Rhines, if you've got Sally Hadlock, it's the best day's work you ever did in your life."

"I don't know what you'll say when I tell you the rest of it." He then informed them that he had bought Elm Island, and was going to live on it.

"But, Ben, is Sally willing to go on that island to live? I'm sure I should be frightened to death to live there."

"'Twas her own plan. She wouldn't hear to my going to sea; and when I said I didn't know of any way to live ashore, unless I bought that island, she said 'twas just the thing. I was intending to build a frame house next summer; but she says, 'Build a log house, go right into it, and build a frame house when you're better able;' and declares she'll live in a log house, and nothing else. I had money enough, that I got privateering, to have bought the island, and built the house on't; but I felt it my duty to help my father out of his difficulties."

"Goodness! gracious! goodness me!" exclaimed Hannah Murch, holding up both hands. "Ben Rhines, are you a wizard, to bewitch the girls after this fashion? Such offers as that girl has had, to my sartin knowledge! She loves you, Ben, and you may be sure of that to begin with. Well! well! well! this beats all the story books."

"She's just right," said Isaac. "She knows that Ben gives up the cap'in's berth to please her; that he'll have a hard scratch of it, and she means to scratch, too. You're just right, both of you."

"Now, Uncle Isaac," said Ben, "this house must go right up. Will you go on with me and another man, and 'boss' the job?"

"I will, Ben; and I won't turn my back to any body for building a log house."

"To-day is Thursday. I should like to begin Monday, if you can come."

"Well, I don't know anything to hender; if you haven't got anybody looked out to help you, I think you'd better get Joe Griffin; he's a strapping stout feller, handy with an axe, or any kind of tools. I know he'll go; and if you say so, I'll bring him along with me, and we'll be at the landing at sunrise, or thereabouts."

During Ben's absence, the widow Hadlock put on her changeable silk, which her husband bought in foreign parts, and her best cap, and taking her knitting-work, went over to Captain Rhines's. When she came back, she reported that it was all right, and the Rhineses were as much pleased with the match as she was.

CHAPTER VIII.

BREAKING GROUND ON ELM ISLAND.

MONDAY morning came, and in the little cove, abreast of Captain Rhines's door, lay moored a "gundelow," containing some hay, an ox cart, plough, scraper, pot and tea-kettle, and provisions, raw and cooked. Just as the sun rose, Ben came down the hill with a yoke of oxen, and an axe on his shoulder weighing fourteen pounds. Joe Griffin made his appearance on foot, and Isaac Murch on horseback, with his wife (who had come to take the beast back) riding behind him on a pillion. It was a bright October morning; the fields were white with frost, which was just beginning to melt as the sun rose.

"Halloa!" cried Joe, as he caught sight of Ben's head over the rising ground; "this is the weather for the woods; the frost puts the grit in."

Hannah Murch, saying that she was going to see Sally Rhines, that is to be, and would meet them at four o'clock Saturday afternoon, rode off.

They put up a boat's sail in the forward part of the "gundelow," and, as the wind was fair, made good progress. Ben steered, while the others stretched themselves at full length upon the hay.

Joe was half asleep, when he felt his leg grasped by Ben, who motioned him to crawl to him as easily as possible.

"There's a flock of coots to leeward; steer her right down on them, and when they rise I'll give it to them."

He carefully lifted a board, under which lay a gun, with an old flint lock, with a stocking leg over it to keep off the damp of the sea and the mist of the morning. Ben crawled forward behind the hay, where he lay with his finger on the trigger. The unsuspicious fowl kept diving and chasing each other over the water: at length they seemed to take alarm, and began to huddle together.

"They're going to rise, Ben," whispered Joe.

"Well, let them rise."

Coots, when they are fat, cannot well rise from the water, except against the wind. As they rose and flew towards the "gundelow," exposing their most vital parts to a shot, five fell dead, and four wounded.

"There's our supper to-night, at any rate," said Ben; "and were we in

41

anything else than this scow, I'd have those wounded ones."

They reached the island, and luffing round its eastern point, ran the "gundelow" on the beach at the mouth of the cove. Joe, making a leaping-pole of an oar, sprang ashore. "Throw us a rope, and you go astern, and I'll haul her in." While Joe pulled on the rope, Ben stepping overboard, put his little shoulders to the stern of the "gundelow," and shoved her so high up on the beach that Isaac Murch stepped out without wetting his feet.

"I say, Ben," exclaimed Joe, "suppose you take an ox under each arm, and bring them out. I never was here before, but if this ain't just the handsomest place I ever set eyes on. Such a nice little harbor to keep a craft; and a brook, and this little green spot in the lee of the woods; then such a master growth of timber; there's a pine that'll run seventy feet without a limb. I say it's great, I do."

Let us glance a moment at the character and capacities of these three men, as they stand together on the beach of this little gem of the wild Atlantic coast.

They represent the yeomanry of the nation. They are of the old stock; not technically religious men, and yet no word of profanity, or disrespect to religion, finds utterance or countenance from them. That which, in their estimation, is of the greatest importance, is to have something which they have earned with their own hands. Look at them, as they stand there at the water's edge, and know them. Physically considered, they are noble specimens of manly vigor and power.

What would some of the effeminate dandies that throng our streets, or the scions of nobility in the old world, be good for on that wild sea-beach? But these men can live there, and cause others to live, and turn the wilderness into a garden.

Isaac Murch is five feet eleven inches in height, fifty-three years of age, without a gray hair on his head, of powerful, compact frame, with a world of intelligence and kindness in his face, and something about him that, without the least assumption, caused his neighbors to respect his opinion, and look up to him as a leader. His early advantages for learning were very slight; but since he has been in easy circumstances, he has improved strong natural capacities by reading and observation.

Joe Griffin was twenty-two—a boy, as Isaac Murch called him; and a great red-cheeked, corn-fed boy he was, too; six feet in his stockings, and weighing a hundred and eighty pounds; loose-jointed, big-boned, thin in the flanks, not long-legged, but getting his length between his shoulders and his hips. He is of less capacity, and more interested in physical matters. He can read and

42

write, cipher as far as the "rule of three," and cast interest; but he has a knack of handling tools that comes by nature. As the neighbors say, he has an eye,— that is, he can judge of proportions, and, with his great clumsy fingers, do anything with wood that he likes; but his great ambition is, to go ahead and do the work. He's smart, and knows it, and likes to have other people know it. He don't calculate to let anybody go ahead of him with a scythe, or chop into the side of a tree, or put hay on to a cart, quicker than himself. Indeed there were very few that could; for he was not only strong, but tough, and possessed infinite tact, laying out his strength to the best advantage.

Let us consider the type of labor presented to us. Here are three live Yankees, in whom all the shrewd, inventive genius of the race has been stimulated by necessity,—all of them, from early life, having been flung upon their own resources.

They are helping one of their number to build a house for himself and his young wife to live in. One of them has already passed through that experience of life which their employer is about to enter. The other expects to, for he also intends to be married, and have a home and land of his own. They therefore go about their work with interest and sympathy.

How different are these men from what is generally termed *help*! They are hired, to be sure; but the sentiment which inspires their labor is entirely different from that feeling of drudgery, under the influence of which the tenantry of Europe, or even the Irish servants in this country, perform their work.

Isaac Murch is an independent, wealthy farmer,—a mechanic by nature,— who has acquired the property he holds with his own hands, and would scorn to be a hired servant, like an Irish navvy; but for *accommodation*, he will hire some one to get in his own harvest, and in the cold, frosty nights, when he might be comfortable at home in the blankets, he will go on to Elm Island, sweat and work, live rough, and sleep on the ground, to build a house for his neighbor; for *neighbor* meant something in those days.

As for Joe Griffin, he's counting every dollar, and looking forward to the day when he shall have a home of his own, and plough his own acres, and is ambitious to earn his wages.

How superior are the results of such labor, to that of the man who has no ambition of ever being anything more than a servant, and only exercises his ingenuity in getting through the day, and shirking all the work he can! They knew that Ben had nothing but his hands to help himself with, and couldn't afford to pay them for watching the shadows; besides, they had a reputation to sustain, of which they were sufficiently proud. They knew very well that everybody within a circle of ten miles would know what they were about before night, and what remarks would be made about them at the blacksmith's shop, the grist-mill, and around the firesides.

"Well, now, if there ain't a team—Isaac Murch, Ben Rhines, and Joe Griffin! Pine trees'll have to take it now, if they've got Isaac Murch to lay out the work, and Ben and Joe to back him up. Won't they have a good time, though, seeing which is the smartest?"

"Wal, sartainly," exclaimed old Aunt Molly Bradish, "Joe Griffin has met his match for once; he can't do anything with Ben Rhines; he'd pull up a pine tree by the roots, if he took a notion."

"Joe can't, of course, take hold of a log to lift with Ben, nor anybody else in this world," said Seth Warren; "but I'll bet he'll chop into the side of a tree as quick; he strikes so true, he wouldn't miss a clip once in a fortnight. I saw him cut a pig of lead in two, down at the mill; and though he struck ten times, he hit so true that you could see but one mark of the axe."

"Wal," replied Aunt Molly, "there's this to be said of Ben Rhines, that is not to be said of everybody: I took him in my arms when he was born, and have lived a near neighbor to him from that day to this, and I never knew or heard of his using his strength to harm a fellow-critter, except they desarved it most outrageously. I've seen little snipper-snappers impose upon him, and all the same as spit in his face, and he never let on that he heard them. Sally's my own niece, and I set my eyes by her; but I couldn't wish her better luck than to marry Ben. He's helped everybody; I should think somebody might have sprawl enough to get up a 'bee' and help him."

They also knew that, when they went to meeting, Sunday, everybody would want to know how much they'd done. Added to this was the pride of emulation, which leads men of any pluck to exert themselves in the presence of each other. This is a kind of labor that can exist nowhere but in a free country, is the result of its institutions, from which proceed the motives, and a thousand subtle influences which beget it.

The island well merited Joe's encomium. On the eastern side, adjoining the brook, was a large space, having a slight elevation, covered with green grass, extending back to the middle ridge, which, at its extremity, terminated in a perpendicular ledge, which, sloping gradually on the eastern side, and disappearing, crossed the brook, where it again came to the surface, forming a natural dam, about two feet in height, with a little fissure in the middle, worn by the passage of the water. Over this the stream fell with a pleasant murmur, mingling very sweetly with the deeper tone of the breakers. On either side of the brook were two enormous elm trees, united by a great root, flat on the surface, which bridged the brook a very little above the fall. Under this root, which was as large as a man's body, the water had a free passage, except in the spring and autumn, when the brook was swollen by melting snows and rains. Then the old root was half buried in water. The high tides came over this natural dam; and in the brackish water were great quantities of smelts and frost fish; and eels also ran up through the fissure in the ledge. The summit of the high ledge was covered with white birches, the great forked roots, rough and black with whorls and blisters, running along the very edge of the rocks, while their limbs, stretching themselves towards the sun, fell in great masses over its edge.

They are very much mistaken who suppose that no one can appreciate natural beauty, or hold communion with the beautiful forms of nature, and grow by it, who has not graduated at a university and read Homer.

Joe Griffin appreciated the beauty of this spot, and felt it to his heart's core; and so did big Ben, though they could not express it in artistic language.

Ben, in consultation with uncle Isaac, had determined to hew his logs for their whole length only on two sides, which, as it was late in the year, and they were pressed for time, would save much labor; but at the ends, and where the doors and windows were to be, to hew them to a "proud edge." This would give good joints at the ends, and make the house as tight as though it was all square timber.

"Where are you going to set your house?" inquired Uncle Isaac.

"Here," said Ben, walking up to the slope above some elms that grew close together, and sticking down a crowbar; "I want my house under the lee of the woods and the hill, and my garden under that warm ledge."

"How large will you have it on the ground?"

"Thirty-six by thirty-nine."

"Jerusalem!" exclaimed Joe; "that's a big house for two people, and a little yellow dog with white on the end of his tail, to live in; hope you won't be crowded."

"Log houses," said Uncle Isaac, "last some time; perhaps he thinks there'll be more of them before it rots down."

"At first," said Ben, "and perhaps for some years, it'll have to be house, barn, corn-house, workshop, and everything."

"You'll have your cellar under half of it; how high will you have it?"

"I never have thought anything about that."

"Well, I'd drop the beams down, and have it a story and a half; that great chamber'll be the best part of the house; 'twill make you a splendid corn-house; that's the way your grandfather's was, and many a bushel of corn I've shelled in it. If I'm boss, as you, Ben, are strong enough to hold the scraper alone, you and Joe can take the plough, and go to ploughing and scraping out the cellar, and I'll go to the woods and pick out and cut the trees."

"The sun is getting low," said Ben; "it is time we were making calculations for sleeping to-night, whether in the 'gundelow,' with a sail over us, or in a bush camp."

"I go in for the bush camp," said Uncle Isaac.

"And I'm the boy to build it," said Joe; "takes me to do that."

"Go ahead, Joe, and build it, and we'll get the wood for the fire."

Without a moment's hesitation, Joe went into the edge of a little clump of bushes, and in a few minutes cut out a space about twelve feet square, leaving an opening between two trees, where he went in, of about three feet. As fast as he cut the trees, he thrust them back, and jammed them in among the others, making a thick wall; he then wove two or three small trees in on the side to keep them from falling in. He then cut three or four small beech limbs, twisted them into withes, bent down the tops of three or four trees on the sides, tied them together with the withes, thus forming the roof; then getting the boat's sail, threw it over the top, and a little brush over that, to break the force of the rain. He then strewed some hemlock brush on the floor to sleep on.

"I'll risk any rain-storm driving us out of that," said Joe, contemplating his edifice with great satisfaction.

"I must have a door," said Joe, "or these plaguy oxen and sheep'll be in there when we ain't, and bother us."

You may think this a difficult matter, but Joe never wasted a thought on't. He took three spruce poles, as long as the height of the opening, drove them into the ground, and wattled them with birch limbs; he then fastened a pole across each end, and one in the middle, leaving the middle one protruding about four inches on the right side; that was a latch. He now took a little hemlock, peeled the bark off, and drove it into the ground on the left side; this was the door-post. He made hinges of withes, which slipped easily round the smooth pole. On the right hand tree grew a limb, slanting upwards; this he cut off about three inches from the tree; then lifting the door, he threw it into the angle, and it was shut and latched.

He drove two crotch-poles into the ground, just before the door, and put another across; he then cut a limb with a side branch growing out of it, and hooked it over the pole; cut a deep notch in the lower end of it, to receive the bail of the pot, and hung it on.

Uncle Isaac and Ben now came with a whole cart full of dry wood, which they had picked up, and a fire was kindled. It was not long before the flavor of the coot stew saluted their nostrils.

"O, that smells good," said Joe; "I'm savage hungry." Seizing his axe, he cut some great chips out of the side of a tree, which he hollowed out, and giving one to each, said, "There's the plates; they don't need any washing; you can shie them into the fire when you're done; there's enough more where they come from."

The stew was now taken from the fire, and these hardy men, who had shown so much capacity for labor during the day, manifested no less for eating. When the solid contents of the stew had disappeared, Joe exclaimed, "I think it's too bad to lose all this good gravy in the pot." He went to the beach and got three clam-shells; these they stuck in the end of split sticks, and soon despatched the contents of the pot.

"Well," said Uncle Isaac, as they stretched themselves around the blazing fire, "we've got on here, made a beginning, and got to housekeeping; and that will do pretty well for one day. We couldn't expect to make much show to-day; but to-morrow we shall get to work betimes, and bring more to pass."

"I'm sorry I forgot to bring a drag," said Ben; "we've nothing to haul the rocks on."

"That's a thing we must have," said Uncle Isaac; "I'll make one right off."

"You can't make it to-night," said Ben.

"The dogs I can't. Joe, cut that little red oak; you can do it in three minutes. Make a blaze, Ben, to see to work by; then run to the 'gundelow,' and bring up that plank I saw there."

By the time Ben returned with the plank the tree was down.

"Now, Joe," said Uncle Isaac, "you can take one side of the tree, and I will the other, and see if you can keep up with your grandfather. You, Ben, may saw up that plank into pieces three feet long, and make some wooden pins."

By nine o'clock the drag was made.

"There," said Uncle Isaac, "that hasn't killed anybody; 'twould have been an awful waste to have taken good daylight for that. I'm not sure but 'twould have been a sin; and we've plenty of time left to sleep."

Thursday was occupied in framing together the sills, and laying the lower floor, in order that they might have it to stand on while rolling up the logs. It was left rough, because Uncle Isaac said it would wear smoother than if 'twas planed.

"I hope," said Joe, "it won't be like old Uncle Yelf's floor. He had a floor of hemlock boards, rough from the saw; they had a heap of grandchildren, every one of them barefoot. Go in there when you would, for a fortnight, there'd be old granny with her darning-needle, and a great young one's foot up in her lap, a-picking out the splinters, while the young one, with both hands on the floor, was screaming bloody murder. By the time she'd picked the splinters out of his feet, there'd be as many more in his hands."

Saturday forenoon was spent in hauling logs, and rolling them up on skids, preparatory to hewing.

Just as they had finished dinner, Joe suddenly cried, "What's that in that bushy spruce on the edge of the bank?"

"I don't see anything," said Ben.

"Nor I, now; but I know there was something there, and I believe it's there now."

"Perhaps it's a coon," said Uncle Isaac.

"A coon? How could a coon get on to this island?"

"How could he get here? How could the squirrels and woodchucks get here? God Almighty put 'em here."

Going to the tree, Joe peered a long time among the branches; at length he exclaimed, "Here he is: get your gun, Ben!"

"I shot away the last powder I had to kindle fire this morning; but we'll stone him down."

They pelted him with stones in vain, the thick limbs causing them all to glance.

"Climb up and get him, Joe."

"Climb up yourself, Ben; they say their bite's rank 'pizen.'"

"I'll have that coon," said Ben, "if it takes all day. Cut the tree down, Joe."

As it fell, the coon leaped from it; and though the stones fell thick and fast around him, he ran up the bank and under the logs. Then began a most exciting race, the men rolling the logs here and there, and striking at him between them, till finally he broke cover, and ran for the woods, with the whole scout at his heels. Ben overtook him just as he was running up a tree, and, catching him by the tail, flung him over his head: he landed on Joe's back, who, having a mortal terror of the bite of a coon, roared with agony; but the creature, too frightened to bite, rolled off his back to the ground, and passing Uncle Isaac, who was so full of tickle that he could not lift a finger to stop him, ran under the timber again. As he was now too far gone to try another race for the woods, he hid under a log, one end of which lay upon a block, and the other on the ground.

Ben saw his eyes shine, and kicked the log off the block; as the coon attempted to run out, it fell on his tail and held him fast. There he sat, captive but undismayed, showing his white teeth, and frothing at his mouth with pain and rage.

"How are you, coonie?" said Joe, taking off his hat and making a low bow; "by the chances of war you are now our prisoner; we are cannibals, of the cannibal tribe, and eat all our captives; you must die for the good of the tribe;" and thus saying he knocked him on the head.

"I'll get mother to bake him to-night," said Ben; "come over to-morrow, Joe, and help eat him."

"Boys," said Uncle Isaac, "don't you think we look well skylarking at this rate? and to-day is Saturday, too; now we must put in hard enough to make up for it."

They labored till dark, as if their lives depended on it.

"I thought you were going to leave off earlier Saturday night," said Hannah Murch, as she met them at the landing. "I've been waiting here more'n two hours in the cold. I was afraid some accident had befallen you."

Ben held up the raccoon.

"I see how it is; you've been cooning, and had to work later to make it up. Isaac, I do wish you would ever leave off being a boy."

"Well, you're the first woman I ever heard of that wanted her husband to grow old."

CHAPTER IX.

TOO GOOD A CHANCE TO LOSE.

BEN persuaded Joe Griffin to go home with him, stay all night, and help eat the coon. Though one of the most kind-hearted creatures that ever lived, Joe's proclivity for practical jokes was both instinctive and inveterate. If the choice lay between making a mortal enemy for life and a good joke, he could not prevail upon himself to forego the joke. He was very shrewd withal, and would extricate himself from difficulties, and accomplish his ends by pleasantry, where others would be compelled to fight their way out, or miss of their object.

One autumn, the blacksmith, having great quantities of axes to make for the loggers, hired Joe a couple of months, as there was a great deal of striking with the sledge, and his apprentice was young and light. The smith was a very driving man, but kept his men well, and was very hospitable. He was obliged to be absent occasionally to deliver his axes. At such times his wife, who was penurious in the extreme, kept the boys very short. Joe, knowing that his master did not approve of this, resolved to put a stop to it. They worked evenings. One night the smith came home full of grit, as he had been riding and resting, and prepared to forge an axe. Placing a hot iron on the anvil, he cried, "Strike, Joe, strike." Joe struck a few feeble blows, when exclaiming, "It's going! it's going! it's all gone!" dropped his sledge on the floor, and seemed ready to faint away.

"What's gone?" cried the smith, in a rage at having lost his heat.

"That water porridge we had for supper."

The master then took them to the house, and gave them a hearty meal.

Once more the iron was laid upon the anvil; Joe struck tremendous blows, making the sparks fly all over the shop, crying, "It's coming! it's coming! it gives me strength! I feel it! I feel it!"

"What's coming, and what do you feel?"

"That good beefsteak I had for supper."

Joe could talk like anybody under heaven, and look like them too. He could talk more like Uncle Sam Yelf than Uncle Sam could himself. This gift, however, he used very sparingly, for he could take a joke as well as give one;

felt that 'twas mean to turn the peculiarities of others into ridicule, and in a way in which they could not retaliate.

Yelf had a sort of hitch in his voice, which was very ludicrous, but, like many people who have an impediment, could sing distinctly and shout tremendously; he was also very hot in his temper. Sometimes, when they met at the store, Joe would begin to talk with him, and just like him.

The old man would fly in a passion in a moment, begin to sputter, and Joe would "take him off," while no human being could help laughing. It was fine sport for the young folks, and the more so on account of its rarity, as it was but seldom that Joe could be persuaded to do it, and was sure to give the old man some tobacco soon after. He could also imitate the cry of any beast, wild or tame, to perfection, from a moose to a muskrat; and of birds, except the squawk; Joe said the squawks were too many for him.

This power was of great value to him in hunting. He could call a moose or muskrat within range, by imitating the notes of either.

In the evening Ben went over to the widow Hadlock's. He was in the habit of making a bootjack of the crane; standing on one leg, and steadying himself by the mantel-piece, he put the other foot into the crotch of the crane, and pulled off his boot. Joe had often seen him do this, and laid his plans accordingly. After the family were all asleep, Joe got up, and with a crowbar pulled out the dogs that held the crane, and then put them back again in such a manner that the least touch would loosen them, and bring crane and all on to the floor. He then took a cow-bell from a cow's neck in the barnyard, and putting some stones in an old tin pail, hung them and a bottle of sour milk on the crane, and went back to bed.

About twelve o'clock Ben came. He felt round for a candle, expecting to find it where his mother usually left it—on the mantel-piece; but Joe had taken very good care to remove both candle and matches; so, feeling for the crane, he clapped in his foot and pulled; down came the crane on to the floor. Ben went over backwards, full length on the floor, with a force that shook the whole house from garret to cellar; the cow-bell and tin pail rattled; the sour milk ran all over Ben; his mother awaked from a sound sleep, and screamed murder; and old Captain Rhines came rushing out in his night-shirt, with a pistol in each hand, blazed away at the sound, putting one bullet through the window, and the other into a milk-pan of eggs, which stood upon the dressers, while the children, roused by the frantic screams of the mother and the pistol shots, came shrieking from their beds.

"Don't shoot any more, father," cried Ben; "it's me."

"My God!" exclaimed Captain Rhines, feeling the milk, which, by hanging over the fire, had become warm, as it touched his bare feet, and mistaking it for blood; "have I shot my own son?"

"No, father," said Ben; "it's some of that confounded Joe Griffin's work. I'll fix him." He ran up stairs to take summary vengeance. In this he was disappointed, for the moment Joe heard the crash, he slid down on a pole, which he had previously placed at the window, and ran home.

We must remember that Ben had been courting; had on his best broadcloth, purchased on the last voyage, and in which he was to be married.

Broadcloth suits in those days were limited to a very few. The minister had a coat and breeches for Sabbath; so of a few of the seafaring people and their families; but the clothing of the people in general was both manufactured and made up at home, there being no such thing as a tailor.

Here, then, was Ben's best suit, made in Liverpool by a professional tailor, soaked with sour milk, and covered with ashes; his light buff waistcoat all over smut, from the pot, crane, hooks, and trammels, that fell over him. Thus, though Ben's temper was not easily roused, and soon subsided, he was now thoroughly mad, and, had he caught Joe, would probably have crippled him for life. Perhaps some such thought crossed his mind, as he said to his father on coming down, "He's gone, and I'm glad of it; but I'll be even with him before snow flies."

Aunt Molly Bradish's declaration that Ben Rhines had helped everybody that needed help, and that she should think somebody might give him a lift, was not lost. Seth Warren happened to be in there, and heard the old lady's remarks. Seth was a kind-hearted, jovial fellow, who had been many a time with Ben on his errands of mercy, and loved any kind doings. He went directly to the store, where, as he expected, he found, as it was Saturday night, a good portion of the young men of the place assembled. He took them aside, and said, "You know what a good fellow Ben Rhines is; how he has always been getting up 'bees' to help everybody that was behindhand: now, what say for going on to the island next week, the whole crew of us, and giving him a lift with his house?"

Seth's proposition was received with acclamations. "Now, boys," he continued, "you know how such things always leak out, and that spoils the whole. Now, don't say a word about it to neither sister, mother, or sweetheart, till they have gone back to the island Monday morning, and then we can talk as much as we please, and they cannot possibly get wind of it."

This was solemnly assented to.

"I," said Seth, "will go over and sleep with Joe Griffin Sunday night, and, without letting him suspect anything, find out how far they've got along with their work, that we may know when our help will be most needed." This he did, when Joe told him what he did the night before at Captain Rhines's.

"What do you suppose Ben'll do to you? He'll murder you after he gets you on to the island. I shouldn't want to be in your shoes."

"Poh! he won't, neither; he's like a bottle of beer, soon up and soon over. I think it is like enough he'll throw me overboard; if he does, I don't care; I'd be willing to be ducked twenty times for the sake of the fun I had that night, and for the better fun I shall have thinking about it and telling of it."

The next morning Seth accompanied Joe to the shore; but no sooner was the gundelow fairly off, than getting on the horse with Hannah Murch, who had come to bring her husband, he let out the whole matter to her. Hannah, by no means backward in the good work, told everybody she met on the road, and went to the school-house and told the mistress.

The result of this was, that thirty-five young men agreed to go,—among whom were ten ship-carpenters from Massachusetts, who were there cutting ship timber, with their master workman, Ephraim Hunt; also, Sam Atkins, from Newburyport, who was at home on a visit.

The girls, under the direction of Hannah Murch, were to cook and furnish the provisions, while John Strout engaged to set them on in his fishing schooner, the Perseverance, an Essex pink-stern, of sixty tons.

CHAPTER X.

THE SURPRISE PARTY.

WEDNESDAY morning the axes were flying merrily, as Ben and his crew were busy at their timber, when they were startled by a tremendous cheer, and, to their utter amazement, beheld thirty-five men, in military order, emerging from the woods, led on by Seth Warren, with a three-cornered cap, in which were the tail feathers of a turkey, with a skein of yarn for a sash, and shouldering an adze. Each man was armed,—some with broad-axes, others narrow-axes, saws, augers, and other tools.

When Seth had marched his men up in front of the cellar, he commanded them to stand at ease.

It is impossible adequately to describe the amazement of the party on the island. Joe stood leaning on his axe, with his mouth wide open; Uncle Isaac held his hat before him with both hands, as if for a shield; while Ben, who had, under the first impulse, started forward to meet Seth, unable to get any farther, stood with both hands in his pockets, the picture of astonishment and doubt.

"Now, Ben," exclaimed Seth, with a magnificent flourish of his hand, and very much at his ease, while his eyes were dancing in his head with suppressed glee, as he noticed the completeness of the surprise, "did you suppose there were never to be any more 'bees,' and that folks wan't going to help each other any more, because you are going to be married, and have got through with it? I tell you, you've learnt us the trade, and we've come to practise, and help the fellow that has set us so good an example—ain't we, boys?"

Seth's speech was received with a cheer. Poor Ben, feeling that he must say something, and not knowing what to say, presented a most ludicrous picture. His great body swayed to and fro; he stood first on one foot and then on the other, to the great delight of his friends, who were in high glee at this evidence of the thoroughness of the surprise.

At length the great creature, who would have faced a battery without winking, blurted out, "Neighbors, I—'m—sure, I don't know what I've done to deserve all this kindness," and burst into tears.

"Don't know what you've done?" replied Seth, anxious to cover Ben's confusion; "*I* should like to know what you *haven't* done. Who raised a scout, and built Uncle Joe Elwell a barn, after his'n was struck by lightning?"

"Who," said John Lapham, "got in the widow Perry's harvest, and cut all her winter's wood, after her husband was killed stoning a well?"

"Ah!" exclaimed John Strout, the skipper of the Perseverance, "who was it took care of me when I had the smallpox in Jacmel, and everybody else, even my own relation, run away from me?"

"Well," replied Ben, whose modesty revolted at such a display of his virtues, "I didn't do any more than my duty."

"That's just what we're going to do," replied Seth.

"And that's where you're right," said Uncle Isaac, putting on his hat. "Come on, boys; if you're so anxious to work, I'll give you enough of it to start the grease out of you."

"Let you alone for that, uncle," said a voice from the crowd.

"Who's that? As I'm alive it's my nephew, Sam Atkins. Where did you drop from, Sam?"

"Why, you see, uncle, we were waiting for timber at Newburyport, that is to come in a vessel; and as Jacob Colcord was coming down in his schooner, I thought it would be a good time to make a visit home."

"You couldn't have done a better thing; you're just the boy I want. Now, Master Hunt, if you'll be good enough to line these timbers for these boys to hew, I'll be doing something else."

Sam Atkins, who was well assured his uncle would not overlook his capabilities, sat on a log whittling. After he had set all the rest to work, Uncle Isaac came to him, and laying his hand upon his shoulder, said, "Sam, I've got a nice job for you; I want you to frame the roof; you'll find tools in my tool-chest. There are the rafters, and they will have the ridge-pole and purlins hewed by the time you will want them."

As soon as a good number of sticks were hewed, they began to roll them up, while Uncle Isaac, Joe Griffin, and two of the ship carpenters, cut the dovetails. By twelve o'clock they had the timber for the walls hewed, and the walls raised to the chamber, and the beams and sleepers for the chamber floor hewed, and Sam and his crew had the roof framed.

In order to make the surprise to Ben complete, they had anchored the schooner behind the woods, on the north-east end of the island; but they now brought her round, and anchored her in the cove, and brought ashore their provisions—jugs of coffee all made, with the sweetening boiled in; cheese and doughnuts, bread and butter, beef, pork, and lamb, all cooked, which the girls had provided; and a good deal more raw, which they meant to have the fun of cooking themselves.

They laid some boards on logs, and thus made their tables.

After dinner, they lay on the grass and talked and laughed, while the older ones smoked, and had a jolly good time.

At length Uncle Isaac said, putting his pipe in his waistcoat pocket, "Boys, do you calculate on having a frolic in the house to-night?"

"Yes, we do," replied a score of voices.

"Then it's high time you were laying the chamber floor."

"You old drive," said Joe, speaking thick, with the ribs of a sheep between his teeth, "didn't you know old Captain Hurry is dead? cast away, going down to Make Haste? Can't you give a feller time to eat? That's been the way ever since I've been here, boys. I'm getting quite thin."

"He don't show it much," said Uncle Isaac, pointing to Joe's fat cheeks; "he has had an hour and a half, and eaten almost a whole sheep."

As nothing was planed except the edges of the floor boards, and what was absolutely necessary to make the joints, the work went on "smoking."

"Ah," said Uncle Isaac, stopping to draw a long breath, while the sweat dropped from the end of his nose on to the axe handle, "that's the time of day, my bullies; all strings are drawing now."

In a short time Joe sung out that the floor beams were all laid, cross sleepers in, and they wanted something to do to keep them from freezing.

"Well, lay the rough floor, and be quick about it; the boards are all jointed, and we shall be at your heels with the upper one."

By the time Joe and his crew had laid half of the loose floor, the ship carpenters began to lay the other one over it, and they finished nearly at the same time.

There were two courses of logs above the floor beams, so that the house was a story and a half in height. The logs being hewn on two sides, then smoothed with an adze, the window frames fitted close, the walls two feet or more in thickness, and very few windows, the house was almost as tight as though it grew there.

"Hand that timber right up here," shouted Uncle Isaac, from the chamber floor, "and clap the roof on. That'll be enough for one day; there's reason in all things."

As there were half a dozen men to a rafter, the timber went up in a few moments.

CHAPTER XI.

THE CHRISTENING.

"HALLOA, Uncle Isaac!" shouted Joe from the house-top, "this ridge-pole won't fit; you didn't make it right."

"Yes, I did. I never made a bad joint in my life."

"Well, it won't fit, anyhow. Master Hunt says 'twont."

"O, if I could only get a little spirit to rub on it," said Uncle Isaac, in great perplexity, "I'll bet 'twould fit; but I'm sure I don't know how I can get it on this island."

"There's some aboard the schooner," said John Strout; and, as it was passed up the frame, Joe announced that the ridge-pole fitted first rate.

"Now, boys, the frame is up, and must be named. Who shall name it?"

"Seth Warren," was the cry; "he got up the scrape." Seth, all at once, became extremely diffident, and required as much urging as a distinguished man at Commencement dinner, but finally was prevailed upon, at a great sacrifice of his own feelings, to gratify his friends. With a bottle of rum in his right hand, and astride the ridge-pole, he gave vent to the following effusion: —

> Here, in the woods, yet out at sea,
>
> Where robins sing amid the surf,
>
> Where ivy clasps the moss-grown tree,
>
> And flowers are breaking from the turf,—
>
> We've reared, where house ne'er stood before,
>
> Nor reaper bound the swelling grain,
>
> A dwelling-place, amid the roar
>
> Of waves, that break to break again.
>
> Good luck to those who here shall live,
>
> Prosperity their path attend,
>
> With every blessing Heaven can give—

Health, competence, till life shall end.
   To them its wealth may ocean yield,
     The herds their milky tribute pour;
   Rich harvests crown the fertile field,
     A bouncing baby grace the floor.
   So strong a man ne'er held a plough,
     A seaman tried, a shipmate true;
   So sweet a girl ne'er milked a cow,
     Or bleached her linen in the dew.
   This goodly house yet lacks a name;
     Good people all, I pray you tell,
   How I most worthily the same,
     This afternoon, may christen well.
   We'll not forget, where'er we roam,
     When thirty-five young stalwart men,
   And Uncle Isaac, reared the home
     Of old Elm Island's Lion Ben.
   I name it, then, the "Lion's Den;"
     When we are dead these walls shall last,
   To tell of times when men were men,
     And keep the record of the past;—
   When worth, not wealth, won woman's heart,
     While she her lighter burden bore;
   At wheel and loom performed her part,
     And added to the common store.

As he concluded, he dashed the bottle on the ridge-pole, and flung the neck high in the air. Seth was frequently interrupted with applause; but, when he finished, there was a complete storm of cheers.

"I call that the cap-sheaf," said Uncle Isaac; "there's some chaw to that; it's raal sentimental; none of your low blackguard stuff, such as they generally have to raisin's. I think we ought all join together, and get Squire Linscott, the town clark, to copy them are varses, and buy a gilded frame, and have 'em hung over Ben's fireplace; then our grandchildren will know about it, for we haven't done anything on this island we're ashamed of, and don't mean to."

It was universally agreed that after such an effort a man must be thirsty; and a large pail of milk punch appeared from the schooner. Seth, as the poet of the day, received the first draught; then Uncle Isaac and Master Hunt, and so it went round.

"It is not near night yet," said Seth, who was greatly pleased with his successful effort; "what do you say for boarding the roof and ends? there is such a swarm of us that we can do it in less than an hour."

"I think we have done enough," said Uncle Isaac; "but I'm in for it if you are."

They accordingly boarded the roof and the ends.

"Now," said Seth, "for some fun."

The chips were all cleared out of the house, and the floor swept with spruce boughs; it made a noble hall; not a thing in it, and almost square. Uncle Isaac, rolling a log in front of the house, sat down to smoke, contemplating his workmanship with the greatest complacency. His thoughts were also occupied in preparing for the morrow. He was desirous of making the most of this godsend, but did not want the boys to feel that he and Ben were trying to get all they could out of them. They had come to work, but for a good time as well. This was the secret of his influence over the boys. He had not outlived his youthful feelings; knew theirs, and liked to frolic as well as they did. Knowing that Seth and Joe were leaders of the rest, and would do anything in reason for Ben, the wise old man determined to create a public sentiment, and then follow the leadings of it; so he took them aside, and told them this plan, of which they highly approved, and which Seth was to propose at the proper time, and Joe to advocate. Seats were now made along the walls; a great quantity of pitch knots were piled up on the foundation of the chimney, and set on fire. This made such a light, that the very heads of the nails in the floor were visible, while the smoke went out of the hole left in the roof for the chimney.

CHAPTER XII.

THE "PULL UP."

"As we can't have any kissing without the girls," said Joe, "let's play 'Pull up.'"

The handle of one of the axes was knocked out, and the game began. It was a most severe test of strength. Two of the company, sitting upon the floor, and putting the soles of their feet together, took hold of the axe-handle, and endeavored to pull each other up. If either broke his hold he was adjudged beaten. Victory in this game depends not merely upon weight, as it might seem at first, but upon strength in the hands, and power of endurance. A man may be very heavy, and have great strength in his arms, and not be strong in his fingers to retain his hold upon the axe-handle.

The young men would sit there and pull, with their teeth set, and the perspiration streaming down their faces, and their eyes almost starting from their sockets. When they were pretty equally matched, one would raise the other from the floor an inch or two, and then lose it again, as his opponent made desperate efforts, and recovered the ground, their friends meanwhile encouraging either party; and as the weakest men were brought on first, and afterwards the strongest and most equally matched, the game became, towards the close, most intensely interesting.

Joe Bradish had pulled up four of his opponents, and being a very conceited fellow, strutted about the floor, and challenged the crowd to pull him up. The challenge would not have remained long unaccepted, but the contest had now become limited to a few of the strongest men, who, knowing they were to be pitted against each other, were saving themselves for the final struggle.

Uncle Isaac saw how it was; and, as he wished to see how the sport would go on, and to teach the braggart a little modesty, he rose up, threw off his outer garment, and accepted the challenge. His proposal was received with shouts of laughter.

"I'm sorry he's done it," said Seth to Joe Griffin, "though I can't help laughing. I should be sorry to see him pulled up before this crowd, for I know it would mortify him; he is just as much of a boy as any of us."

"He won't be pulled. Uncle Isaac, I can tell you, is an all fired strong man;

it don't lay in Joe Bradish's breeches to pull him up."

"I know that; but he's getting in years."

"He can't wrestle and jump quite as well as he could once; but he can lift as much, and pull up as well, as ever he could. Joe Bradish will get a good lesson; he'll never hear the last of it as long as he lives."

"Well, boys," said Uncle Isaac, "fling on some pitch knots; if I am going to be beat, I want everybody to see it."

"What did I tell you?" said Joe, giving Seth a poke in the ribs; "the old man knows what he's about."

The two champions sat down.

"Say when you're ready, Joe," said Uncle Isaac.

"Ready," says Joe.

Uncle Isaac was not only strong, but of very quick strength; and before the words were well out of the other's mouth, he pulled him over his head, into Joe Griffin's arms, who was eagerly looking over Uncle Isaac.

"It ain't fair," said Joe, his face as red as fire; "I wasn't ready."

"You said you was."

"Well, I thought I was; but I wasn't."

"Try it again," was the cry. They sat down. Uncle Isaac waited patiently till Joe had spit on his hands, and said he was completely ready, when he pulled him up just as easily as before.

"I thought you was some, Joe," said Uncle Isaac; "but you ain't nothing."

John Strout, a large, muscular man, whose occupation as a sailor had the effect to concentrate strength in the fingers and chest, had pulled up all who opposed him. The call was now for Joe Griffin, as no one thought of pulling with Rhines. Joe came forward at the summons. Severe was the struggle; and, as these were the last antagonists, the interest was proportionally great. Joe finally pulled John from the floor, but the blood spun from his nose in consequence of his efforts; and John was so exhausted that he could scarcely stand.

"I could not have done it, John, if you had taken hold of me when you were fresh, for an ounce more would have broken my hold."

Uncle Isaac now gave the wink to Seth, who said, loud enough for everybody to hear, "I think it's a pity, now we're here, that we couldn't shingle the house, and build Ben a hovel to put his cow in, and hang the doors; then all he would have to do would be to get married."

"Well, we would do it, if we had the shingles to do it with—wouldn't we, boys?" said Joe Griffin.

"Yes," was the reply from twenty voices; "and we'll build the hovel and hang the doors, at any rate; we've got all the materials for that."

"Well, boys," said Uncle Isaac, "since you are so free-hearted, I'll tell you what I've been thinking of, for I feel about nineteen, since I pulled up Joe Bradish. I've been thinking I should like first rate to have a clam bake."

"A clam bake! a clam bake!" was the cry.

"But then, you see, we have no hoes to dig clams with; and we want some eggs, potatoes, and apples to bake with them. Now, I've got a whole lot of hemlock bark on the edge of the bank on my point, where you can go to it with the gundelow—enough to cover three such houses. I'll lend it to Ben, and when he peels bark next June he can pay me; and I've got nails likewise. If we can get an early start in the morning, we can do the whole, clam bake and all. The bark is all piled up, so that it is flat, and will lay first rate; it will make as tight a roof as shingles, and last seven or eight years, and by that time Ben can make his own shingles. Some of you can load the gundelow, and some can get the hoes and nails; and tell Hannah to give you some corn that grows in the western field,—it's a late piece—the frost hasn't touched it yet, —it's just right to roast; and also get all the apples, eggs, and potatoes you want."

Uncle Isaac's plan met with a hearty approval; and they brought in some brush, and lay down to sleep.

The next morning, at daybreak, John Strout, with a strong party, started after the bark, taking a jug of coffee and a cold bite with them.

The others went to work making preparations to cover the roof of the house, and build the hovel. Uncle Isaac gave Joe Griffin a gang, and set him to build the hovel. Sam Atkins, with the ship carpenters, went to work upon the doors, while the rest put up the staging upon which to work while covering the roof.

The hovel was built of round logs, notched together, with a roof on one side,—what is called a half-faced cabin,—just high enough to clear the cattle's backs, and large enough to hold a cow and yoke of oxen. Nothing was hewed except the poles that made the floor, which were flatted on the upper side; and the openings between the logs filled with clay and mortar.

The crew now arrived with the bark, when, who should come with them, but Uncle Sam Yelf and Jonathan Smullen! Yelf was seventy, Smullen seventy-five. The old men wanted to share in the clam bake, have a little milk punch, and, above all, to witness the wrestling: they had both been champions of the ring in their day.

All hands, except the carpenters, now joined in putting on the sheets of bark; they were lapped like shingles, and, being four feet in length, were laid with great rapidity.

"There are more of you here than can work to advantage," said Uncle Isaac; "some of you, dig clams."

In the mean time the carpenters hung the doors. The hinges and latches were all made of wood. The latch was lifted by a leather string, which was put through a hole in the door above it, and hung down on the outside. Thence came the phrase, "the latch-string out," to denote open doors and hospitality; since, when it was pulled in there was no entrance.

"What on airth," said Uncle Isaac, "has become of Sam Atkins? I haven't set eyes on him this whole forenoon."

While the rest were preparing for the clam bake, he went everywhere looking for Sam. A great fire was now built in the hollow of a ledge, till the rocks were red hot. Into this were put the clams, together with eggs, potatoes, and corn with the husk on; the whole was then covered with sea-weed, to keep in the steam while they were cooking.

There was a short log left in the building of the house, and, in order to pass the time away, while waiting for the dinner, they dug it out, and made a hog's trough: thus Ben's *first* article of furniture was a hog's trough.

The clams formed the first course; eggs, corn, apples, and cheese, the second; concluding with milk punch, which passed from hand to hand in a tin quart.

If ever there was real enjoyment, it was to be found among that frolicsome throng of young men, conscious that they had done a noble act, and, in aiding a neighbor, had found the purest happiness for themselves.

CHAPTER XIII.

INJURED PEOPLE HAVE LONG MEMORIES.

As Ben had shown no disposition to retaliate for the joke played upon him, had never mentioned it to any one, or ever alluded to it, Joe supposed that, with his usual good nature, he had forgotten it.

Ben, on the contrary, had resolved to pay Joe in his own coin, with usury, whenever a fitting opportunity presented itself.

Some weeks before he had mown some tall grass, which grew on the beach, made it into hay, and enclosed it with a brush fence, to protect it from the sheep. Adjoining the stack was a honey-pot. Honey-pots are mires, sometimes twenty feet or more in depth, composed of a blue, adhesive mud, which, by the constant soaking of some hidden spring, and the daily flow of the tide, is kept in a half fluid state, except upon the surface, where the clay, being somewhat hardened by the sun at low water, is stiff, and will bear a man to walk over it quickly; but, if he stands a moment, down he goes.

Joe, who had never been on the island before, was ignorant of the existence of this mire. Ben, while the rest were asleep the night before, had removed all the sand and drift stuff, and scraped the hard clay from the surface of the honey-pot, till it would hardly bear a dog.

While the boys were stretched upon the grass, laughing and talking after dinner, Ben asked Joe to help him bring some hay on the poles for the oxen. When two persons carry hay on poles, the one behind cannot see where he steps, but must follow his leader, who picks the road for him. Ben went as near to the edge of the honey-pot as he dared. The moment he got a little by, he turned short off, bringing Joe right into the middle of it. In he went, carried down both by his own weight and that of the load, clean to his breast, when Ben, twitching the poles away, sat down on the bank to laugh at him.

"O, Ben," cried Joe, "we're square now; help me out."

Ben took out his knife, and began to whittle.

Getting frightened, as he found himself gradually sinking, Joe roared for help, drawing the whole party to the spot. This was just what Ben wanted. He knew that Joe had told everybody in the neighborhood of the trick he put on him, and it was his turn now.

The moment Joe saw Uncle Isaac, he cried out, "Do help me; I'm going down." As there was now real danger of his smothering in the mud, Ben ran the poles under his arms. Joe made desperate efforts to extricate himself by means of the poles, but the mire so sucked him down, that he only succeeded in getting out his shoulders.

At this juncture Tige came rushing along, and, seizing him by the collar, endeavored to lift him out; but sinking down into the slime, which Joe's struggles had wrought into a complete porridge, his mouth and nose were filled with mud and water: giving a vigorous snort, he completely plastered Joe's face and eyes with it, who, not being in the most amiable of moods, hit him a cuff on the side of the head. Tige, enraged at being thus rewarded for his good intentions, was going to bite him, when Ben pulled him away by the tail.

"Pity I wan't a dog," whined Joe; "then there'd be some feeling for me."

He now appealed again to Uncle Isaac; but the old man had thought the matter all over, and come to the deliberate conclusion that it was time Joe's wings were clipped; that, if not checked, he would become unbearable; that there could be no better time to administer reproof, and one stringent enough to be remembered.

"You know, Joseph," said he, in a severe tone, "that the trick you played last week on Ben was not by any means the first you've played on him and others. Who was it put on a bear-skin, got down on all fours, followed the widow Hadlock when she was going home from my house through the woods, and growled, and frightened the poor woman so that she was sick for three months, and the whole town turned out the next day to kill the bear?"

"I cut all her winter's wood, to pay for it."

"Who," said Joe Riggs, "stopped up the chimney, when the young folks had a New Year's party in the chamber over the store, and put peas on the stairs, so that Seth Warren fell from top to bottom, and broke his leg?"

"Joe Griffin," cried Seth.

"He'd done the same to me, if he'd had the chance, and wit enough."

JOE GRIFFIN IN THE HONEY POT. Page 139.

"It makes my heart ache, Joseph," said Uncle Isaac, "to see a young man in your situation in such an unreconciled frame of mind; we never should do wrong to others because they have done, or would do, wrong to us. So far from manifesting any contrition, you justify yourself in your evil courses. Instead of resignation under trial, you appear to me to be 'gritting your teeth,' and thrashing about like unto a seal in a herring net."

"Who was it," asked John Strout, "when Mose Atherton was all dressed up, going to walk round the head of the bay, to see Sally Bannister, offered to show him a shorter cut over the marsh, and led him into a honey-pot, then went to John Godsoe's, told them there was a man's hat on Moll Graffam's honey-pot, and he guessed somebody must be in trouble? When Godsoe's people got there, the tide was flowing around him, and the water up to his chin."

Joe made no reply to this.

"Don't be sullen, Joe, for you must perceive we're measuring you by your own bushel. I begin to fear it may become our duty to leave you here till you're in a more submissive frame of mind."

"O, Uncle Isaac, you won't leave me in this mire, six miles from any human being, to perish?"

"Not to perish, young man, but to repent. Let me see: to-day's Thursday; we can give you a little light food, and leave you over the Sabbath; it's a good day, and should bring serious reflections. The water don't come up here, except when it's a storm. I don't see any signs of a storm—do you, boys?"

The others didn't see much signs of one; some thought that 'twas a little "smurry."

"Reflection is profitable, Joseph. Monday we might find you more reconciled."

"I'll do anything you want me to, if you will only take me out."

"That is better. Will you promise not to play any more tricks upon any of this company, or anybody else?"

"Don't make him lie," said Ben; "he can't help it."

"Well, then, will you promise not to play any more upon any one here, and say that you are sorry for what you did to Ben?"

"I will."

"Then we will take you out; and I trust it will be a warning to you in future. Boys, build up a fire; he must be half perished with cold."

Ben got some boards, and laying them two-thick upon the surface of the honey-pot, walked to the place, and pulled him out; and a miserable plight he was in.

"Jump into the water, Joe," said John Strout, "and wash yourself; and I will go to my chest in the schooner and get you a shift of clothes."

Joe washed the mud off in the water, and then stood by the fire till John came with the clothes; then, putting them on, he washed his own, and hung them on a tree to dry.

"Joe," said Uncle Isaac, "did you see anything of Sam Atkins in that honey-pot? for I'm blest if I know what has become of him."

"Here he comes," said Joe; and, sure enough, he was now seen coming up from the shore, with something on his shoulder.

"What is that, Sam?" asked Uncle Isaac.

"A cradle for that bouncing baby Seth told about." He had got out the stuff unnoticed by the rest of them, and then went on board the schooner and put it together. This was examined by all, and caused abundant jests at Ben's expense.

It was now proposed that they should end the day with a ring wrestle, both at close hugs and arms' length. While the wrestling was going on, the two old gentlemen, for whom a comfortable seat had been provided near the fire, sat looking on, criticising the proceedings, and entering into every detail with intense interest.

The presence of these distinguished veterans, with their great bony frames, —for they had been men of vast pith and power, and famed through all the region,—acted as a mighty incentive to the young men.

"I think, Uncle Jonathan," said Yelf, "you and I have seen the day we could show these boys some things they haven't learned yet. Do you remember that wrastle we had when Captain Rhines's house was raised—there was stout, withy men around these bays in them days;—how you threw Sam Hart, that came forty miles to wrastle with you, and said God Almighty never made the man that could heave him? But he found the man—didn't he?" giving his friend a nudge in the ribs with his elbow.

"They said," replied Smullen, "he was so mortified because he'd bragged so much, that he went home and hung himself. Ah, my toe was so sartin in those days, when I put it in! You know I had a particular trip with my left foot."

"Hoora!" said Uncle Sam, as John Strout crotch-locked Sam Pettigrew, and threw him; "a fair fall that, and no mistake. Both shoulders and both hips on the ground."

The plaudits of the veterans were like fuel to the fire. The young men exerted themselves to the utmost in the presence of such competent judges.

At length their aged blood began to circulate more briskly, under the combined influence of the warm fire, milk punch, and old associations.

"Uncle Sam," said Smullen, "what do you say to me and you trying a fall; we've had hold of one another afore to day?"

"Agreed," was the reply; "but it must be at arm's length. I've had the rheumatics so much that my back's got kinder shackly."

The young people laughed till the tears ran down their cheeks as they stepped into the ring, their upper garments removed, heads bare, and the white locks flowing round their shoulders. Uncle Yelf, producing his snuff-box,—a sheep's bladder,—after taking a pinch, offered it to Smullen, and the contest began.

They exhausted every feint known to the art, and it was soon evident to the young people that these veterans possessed a skill unknown to them, and that it was only in the strength of youth they were lacking.

Beside them was an elm, that separated at the root into two parts. Between the forks Smullen threw Yelf with such force, that he was firmly-wedged, and had to be pulled out.

"Well," said Uncle Sam, "he ought to throw me; he's the oldest."

Just before sunset they took leave of Ben, and, with hearty cheers, made sail.

It was a current saying, in respect to Uncle Isaac, that he could keep more men at work, bring more to pass, with less fuss, and have everybody good-natured, than any man in the district; and nobly had he justified the general verdict.

CHAPTER XIV.

BEN CONFIDES IN UNCLE ISAAC AND IS COMFORTED.

THE party on the island sat by the camp fire, listening to the voices of their departing friends, till they died away in the distance.

"Who are you going to get to build your chimney, Ben?" asked Uncle Isaac.

"Joe Dorset."

"I never'd get him; a poor man can't afford to hire him; he came from Newburyport, and he'd be always heaving out, and telling how much better they have things in Massachusetts; growling about the stuff he has to work with, and can't do anything without merchantable brick."

"I don't know anything about him," said Ben, "only I've heard he is an excellent workman."

"Well, so he is; but when you've said that you've said everything. He'll have a great many long stories to tell, that'll eat up his own time, and hinder other people. I like to hear a good story myself, and tell one too; but I always do it after work, and not to hinder work, in my own time, and not my employer's; besides, he's so lazy! He went fishing one year with John Strout, and he was so long hauling up a codfish that a dogfish eat him all up, and left nothing but the bare hooks to come to the top of the water."

"Who shall I get?"

"Get Sam Elwell."

"He ain't a mason."

"No, but he's a plaguy sight better for your purpose; he's a natural stone layer—took it up of his own head; he'd build you a chimney out of the stones, right here on the island, that'll carry the smoke first rate, and that's all you want of a chimney; and he'll do it in quarter of the time. Then the chimney'll compare with the house, and they'll be all of a muchness."

At this period of the conversation Joe flung himself upon the brush, and was soon sleeping soundly.

"Uncle Isaac, now that we are alone, I want to tell you how I feel. It does seem to me that it's bad enough to bring Sally into a log house at all, and that

I ought, in reason, to have had panel doors in it; more than two windows in the whole in a broadside, with a good brick chimney and oven laid in lime mortar."

"Plank doors, tongued and cleated, are the warmest. Panel doors in a log house would look like a man with a beaver hat on and barefoot. You can cut out a window whenever you like, and the less holes the warmer."

"But the chimney," persisted Ben; "what will she say to that? and how can she get along without an oven?"

"Sally is one that looks into the realities of things; and if she has made up her mind to live on this island, depend upon it she has considered the matter all round, is looking forward to something better, and that will keep her from being discouraged, however severe things may appear at first. I don't suppose as how an *oven* can be made of stone; but I'll tell you what I will do—take up the bricks in my butt'y floor, and lend 'em to you; it's altogether too late for you to get bricks this fall."

"Well, I hope 'twill all turn out well; but I know in my soul that she's no more idea of what living in a log house is, than she has of London."

"I know a great deal more about Sally Hadlock than you do, though you are engaged to be married to her, because I know her people, and there's a great deal in the blood. She is the living picture of her grandmother Hannah, my wife was named for, who came down here when it was a howling wilderness, fought hunger and the Injuns, and beat 'em both. Handsome as she is, and gentle and good as she seems and is, she's got the old iron natur of that breed of folks, who had much rather earn a thing than have it gin to 'em. She's had nothing to call out that grit yet; but you'll find out what she's made of when she comes to be put to't."

"There's one thing that troubles me, that perhaps you haven't thought of. If I was going to take her into a new settlement, where everybody lived in log houses, and all fared alike, it would be another thing; but I am going to bring her where she can look right across the bay, and see the smoke of her mother's chimney, and all her friends and folks living in nice frame houses. Now, if she's unhappy, and keeps it to herself on my account, and grief is gnawing at her heartstrings, I can't bear that."

"Benjamin," said Uncle Isaac, solemnly, who saw his friend was really distressed, "what I'm going to say to you now I say candidly, and what I know to be a fact. I'm a married man, Ben, and know what a woman is. When a woman really sets her heart on a man, he is almost like God Almighty to her; and the more she can put herself out for him, the more contented she is; that is, if she's morally sartin he loves her. Now, Sally loves you with her whole soul, for she might have had her pick of half the young men in town, and she knows it. She is also sure that you love her, or you would never have given up the business prospects that you had, and undergo all that you must undergo on this island just on her account; therefore the more hardships she's called to suffer 'long with you, the lighter hearted she'll be; yes, she'll take pride in't. O, Benjamin, these rich folks, who never know what it is to strive and contrive to get along, don't taste the real honey of married life; they don't know what's in one another, and don't love one another as those do who have to fight for a living. Why, they can't; they haven't had to lean on each other, and be so necessary to each other."

"Well, I never thought of that before."

"Of course, you haven't; I expect you'll have the happiness of finding that out. I tell you, Hannah and I take lots of comfort Sabbath nights, when we ain't tired, talking over all we've been through together. And then sometimes I get the Bible, and read them are varses, where it says, 'She seeketh wool and flax, and worketh willingly with her hands; she will do him good, and not evil, all the days of her life.' I can't help giving her a kiss, and saying, 'Well, wife, I never should've got through it if't hadn't been for you.'"

This last sally of the noble old philosopher of the woods completely silenced Ben, who promised he'd never harbor another doubt in respect to the matter.

"There's another thing, Benjamin; don't try to slick it over any, but make it full as bad as 'tis. If she expects the worst, and then finds it a great deal better'n she expected, 'twill make her more contented. There's a great deal in the first feeling and the first look of a thing, especially to a woman."

The next day Ben and Joe were employed in hauling stone for the chimney, and making clay mortar. Uncle Isaac cut a red oak, and hewed out a mantel-bar, to form the top of the fireplace; it was twelve feet in length, and no less than nine inches square, as it was to support a great weight of stone. Though of wood, it was so far from the fire, on account of the great height and depth of the fireplace, that it could not well burn; besides, it was always the custom, whenever they had a great fire, to wet the mantel-bar the last thing before going to bed.

He then cut a hole through the floor, in what was to be the front entry, to pour potatoes through into the cellar (because the cellar was under the south part of the house), and made a door to cover it.

The house would seem to my readers but a poor place to live in. There were but four windows below, and these being put on the corners, to admit of making others between them when they should be able, gave to the house a funny look. The house consisted of but two rooms below, separated by a rough board partition, in which were two doors of rough boards, hung by wooden hinges. The chamber was reached by a ladder; the boards of the floors were rough, and full of splinters, just as they came from the saw. Against the wall in the north-west corner, with shelves and closets nicely planed, were some dressers to hold dishes. In the cellar was a square arch of stone, into which Uncle Isaac put shelves, and to which he made doors. He then made a cross-legged table, all in one leaf, and a settle to place before the fire, with a back higher than the top of a person's head, to keep off the draughts of air that went up the great chimney.

They went off Saturday, well satisfied with what they had accomplished.

CHAPTER XV.

ENCOURAGING NATIVE TALENT.

THE moment Uncle Isaac landed, he set out for Sam Elwell's. Going along, he saw Yelf's horse feeding beside the road, with the bridle under his feet, and, a little farther on, his master lying in a slough hole, to all appearance dead, but, as it turned out, only dead drunk. He pulled him out, and, as he was unable to stand, set him against the fence to drip, while he caught the horse; his gray hairs and face were plastered with mud; his nose had bled; the blood was clotted upon his beard, and soaked the bosom of his shirt.

"How came you in this mud hole?"

"Why, you see, Isaac, the mare went in to drink; the bridle slipped out of my hand; I reached down to get it, kind o' lost my balance, and fell right over her head, and hit my nose on a rock. I think, Isaac, I must have taken a leetle drop too much."

His friend scraped the mud from him as well as he could with a chip, put him on the mare (for Yelf could ride when altogether too drunk to walk), and left him at his own house, which lay in the direction he was going.

"That's a bad sight," said Uncle Isaac to himself, as he went on, "and it's one that's getting altogether too common. I remember the time when he was content with his three glasses a day, and perhaps a nightcap; but now he can't stop till he stops in a ditch. There ain't a man in this town but what drinks spirit, myself among the rest, and most of them more than's good for 'em. I don't see why people can't use liquor with moderation, and without making a beast of themselves. If it was only these old, worn-out ones, like Yelf, 'twouldn't be so much matter; but it's amongst the young folks; and even boys get the worse for liquor. It's natural they should; for if men sail vessels, boys'll sail boats. It's time something's done, though what can be done I'm sure I don't know. What an awful thing it would be, if, one of these days, Ben or Joe Griffin should pick me out of a ditch, and carry me home to my family looking like that! I'll think about it, and talk with Hannah this blessed night." He was aroused from his meditations by hearing the voice of Sam at his own door.

He was about the age of Isaac, but a much heavier man, being very thick set, with a stoop in his shoulders. His hands were of great size, full of cracks;

his fingers crooked, from constant working with stone hammers and drills; many of the nails jammed off, and his face as hard as the stones he worked on. He was also a man of very few words, while Isaac liked to talk; yet they had been close friends from boyhood, took great delight in each other's society (if it could be called society where one talked and the other listened), and always got together, and worked together, whenever they could. They were both passionately fond of gunning. Isaac was the quicker shot; but Sam could scull a float steadier and faster than any man along the shore. He could also lay brick well, but was possessed of a remarkable gift for working upon rocks. He knew just how to take hold of a great rock to move it, and could do a better quality of work than they ever had occasion for in that rude state of society, where nobody had hammered doorsteps but Captain Rhines, widow Hadlock, and a few others. He knew all about the nature and grain of rocks, could dress underpinning, or make a millstone out of a boulder in the pasture.

He had just come home from a long job, and was taking his tools out of the cart.

"Let them be," said Isaac; "I've got another job for you:" as he spoke he pulled the clevis-pin out of the tongue.

Sam, without a word, unyoked the oxen, and went into the barn to feed them, while the other tied them up.

Isaac, without any invitation, followed Sam into the house. The table was in the floor, and Sam's wife had just put on the victuals. "Set along," said Sam, motioning Isaac to a chair. That's the way they lived. If they chanced to be in each other's houses about meal time, they always stopped. If they met on the road, or were at work together in the woods, or had been off gunning, they always went to the house that was nearest. Their wives never worried about them, for they knew where they were, and were as good friends as their husbands.

"Sam," said Isaac, "did you ever see a fireplace and chimney built of stone?"

"No."

"You didn't?"

"I've seen stones set up in a log camp to build a fire against, with a 'cat and clay' chimney built over them; but 'twas a make-shift till they could get bricks."

"Could it be done?"

"They say Necessity's the mother of Invention. I suppose it might, by putting in the proper stone."

"Well, Ben Rhines has got his house up, can't get bricks this fall, and don't know what to do. He was going to get Joe Dorset to build his chimney; but I told him I knew you could build a good fireplace and chimney out of the rocks on the island, if you had a mind to."

"Dorset don't know anything about rocks," growled Sam.

"Now, let me tell you about the stone. There's a granite ledge on the western p'int that lays in thin sheets, that you can break up with your stone hammer."

"Granite's first rate for a chimney, but 'twont do for a fireplace."

"Then there's a kind of gray stone, with white streaks in it, but softer than granite."

"That's a bastard soapstone; that'll do for a fireplace."

"Well, can you do it?"

"Yes."

"Will you?"

"Yes."

"Enough said. Now, I'm bound Sally shall have an oven; and I'm going to take up my butt'ry floor to make it of."

"You needn't do that. I can make as good an oven of that stone as ever a woman baked bread in. It'll crack some, but not half as bad as granite. It'll hold heat wonderfully."

"You beat all, Sam. I told Ben I knew you could build a chimney without a brick in it; but I never dreamt of your building an oven."

"Who am I to have to tend me, and help handle these big stones?"

"That pretty little Ben Rhines and Joe Griffin, to say nothing of myself."

When Sam went on to the island and saw the stone, he rubbed his hands, and chuckled, and talked to himself, and appeared overjoyed.

"What a queer old coon he is!" said Joe; "anybody'd think he'd found a gold mine, instead of a pile of rocks."

There was but one fireplace, and that was in the kitchen; but the hearths were laid in the two front rooms for two more, whenever they should be parted off and finished.

This fireplace was made of three large stones, which Uncle Sam cut and fitted together without any mortar. It was five feet to the mantel-bar, eight between the jambs, and of proportionate depth. This monstrous cavern was the fireplace. Such a master was Uncle Sam of his business, that when he saw a rock in the pile that he wanted, he would throw a little stone at it, and Ben or Joe would bring it to him.

But it was upon the oven that Uncle Sam displayed his genius. He found a place where a large portion of this bastard soapstone ledge had cracked and fallen out into the sea, leaving a smooth perpendicular face. He told Ben this rock was rent when Christ was crucified. From this ledge he split off just such large, flat slabs as he wanted, made them perfectly smooth, squared the edges, and of them built his oven in the form of a stone box, having top, bottom, and sides of perfectly smooth stones; for he threw sand and water on them, and putting on another great stone, as big as he and Uncle Isaac could lift, he got Ben to scour them, while he stood by and threw on sand and water, till they were perfectly smooth. He now put them together, leaving a space of a foot or more at the sides and ends. The covering stone was made to project on every side, so as to enter into the body of the chimney, in order that, if it should crack, it could not fall down. He now built a roaring fire in it. By and by the great stone on top, and one on the side, cracked with a loud noise.

"Crack away," said Uncle Sam; "crack all you want to."

He then took some clay mortar, filled all the space round the sides, worked it into all the cracks and joints, and, after it was thoroughly dry, made another great fire, and baked it all into brick. It would never crack any more, because the fire had already opened all the bad places in the soapstone, and these were filled with clay mortar, which was now burned into brick.

When the chimney was up to the chamber floor, he made what was called an *eddy*; that is, he brought the chimney right out into the chamber. Across it he put three beech poles, called lug-poles: these were to hang anything on which it was desired to have smoked. He also made a stone shelf in one corner to put an ink-bottle on, or anything that was to be kept from freezing. There was so much fire left on the hearth at night that these great chimneys never got cold. Uncle Isaac then made a tight door, to keep the smoke from coming into the chamber.

"Ben," said Uncle Sam, "are you going to have a crane?"

"No; I can't afford it."

"Then I'll put in another lug-pole."

It was the custom to fasten a chain to this to hang the pot on.

"That's right," said Uncle Isaac, delighted with the effect of his teachings; "a withe is just as good; I'll give you a piece of chain to put on the end of it. When you go up in the spring with a load of spars, you can buy iron, and have a crane made."

"I," said Joe, "will make it for you; I'm blacksmith enough for that."

"Now," said Sam, "I want just one thing—some lime to lay the stone in after I get above the roof, and collar the chimney."

There was a large lot of clam shells on the shore, where the fishermen had shelled clams for bait. These he burned into as handsome white lime as ever you saw. Uncle Sam, though a man of but few words, possessed a very kind heart, and was much attached to Sally; hence the great pains he bestowed upon the chimney and oven. He now, therefore, as the chimney stood right out in the room, and was not concealed by any woodwork, took some of the lime and white-washed it, and also the arch in the cellar. Uncle Isaac now made a fire to try it. It was found to carry smoke splendidly,—upon which he praised it in no measured terms. Sam was evidently much pleased with the encomiums of his friend; and, that both might have cause for satisfaction, Joe then told Sam about Uncle Isaac's pulling up Bradish.

The last thing Uncle Sam did was to split out two large stones for doorsteps. After they were placed, he said to Ben, "These stones are the best of granite; and when you build a frame house, if I ain't dead, or past labor, I'll dress them for you, and they'll make as handsome steps as are in the town of Boston."

"Well, Ben," said Uncle Isaac, as they left the island, "that's a log house; but it's a very different one from those in which your father and I were born and brought up: they were no better than your hovel. We had no cellar, but kept our sass in a hole in the ground out doors. My poor mother never had an oven while she lived, but baked everything on a stone, or in the ashes. She raised a rugged lot of children, for all that, who live in good frame houses, and have land of their own now; but then it's harder for you than 'twas for us, because *we* were all alike, and had never seen anything better; while you are going to live in a log house, right in sight of those who live in better ones. But you will be supported, Ben, and will be prospered."

CHAPTER XVI.

BEN OUTWITTED, AND UNCLE ISAAC ASTONISHED.

SALLY and Ben now began to make preparations for housekeeping. She had a little money, earned by her labor, and she persuaded Ben to go in a schooner that was bound to Salem, and make some purchases for her. No sooner was Ben out of sight, than Sally started for Uncle Isaac's. She found him alone in the barn.

"Uncle Isaac," said she, "will you do something for me?"

"Anything in reason, Sally."

"Could you get me over to Elm Island, and not any soul know it?"

"I suppose I might."

"Well, will you?"

"But what do you want to go there for?"

"I'll tell you. I'm determined to live there, and be contented and happy, and make my husband happy; but I know it will be very different from anything that I have ever seen, or can imagine."

"You'll find it a rough place, Sally."

"I'm afraid that when I go on with Ben I might be kind of surprised, and by looks, if nothing else, show it, and hurt Ben's feelings."

"That you might burst out crying?"

"Yes."

"Well, you go down to the point, and hide in the bushes till I come."

In a short time Uncle Isaac came. Sally got in, and lay down in the bottom of the boat; he covered her over with spruce boughs, and pulled for the island. It was a bright, sunshiny morning. He rowed right into the mouth of the brook, and on to the beach. As Sally felt the boat touch the bottom, she flung off the covering, and, rising up, looked around her.

"What a beautiful spot!" was her involuntary exclamation, as she gazed, enraptured, upon the dense foliage of the maple and birch, rich with all the tints of autumn, and listened to the ripple of the brook that fell over the rocks before her. Then, clapping her hands, she burst into a clear, ringing laugh, as her eye rested upon the house—her future home. Uncle Isaac was confounded. At first he thought it was an hysterical affection, and concealed grief and disappointment; but, as he looked into her eyes, he saw that it was heartfelt. He was in the position of a sailor, who, having braced his yards to meet a squall, is caught aback by the wind coming in an opposite direction. All the way to the island he had been preparing himself for the task of consolation, and arranging his arguments for that purpose,—never for a moment doubting but Sally, with all her resolution, would at first be somewhat disheartened.

"Uncle Isaac," cried Sally, "did that house grow there? See, the bark is on it. What on earth is the chimney made of?"

Then she burst out again into peals of laughter, so joyous that Uncle Isaac joined with her, and laughed till his sides ached.

"Why, Uncle Isaac, Ben told me it was a most desolate-looking place, all woods and rocks; that the house was right on the shore, and that in great storms the sea roared awfully, and the spray would fly on to the windows. He never said a word about the brook. I do love brooks so much! I mean to have my wash-tub, in summer, right under that yellow birch; you see if I don't. Such a nice place to spread out linen thread and cloth to bleach; and things look so much whiter when they are spread on the grass! Why, here is a piece of grass almost large enough for a field; such a sunny, sheltered spot, too! the woods and the hill break off every bit of wind. What a nice place, under that ledge, to plant early potatoes, peas, and beans, and have currant bushes! But I'm dying to see the house; do let us go in; what a nice doorstep this is!"

As they opened the door and went in, Uncle Isaac watched Sally's face in vain to detect any trace of disappointment or sorrow.

She is fire-proof, just like her grandmother, thought he.

"I supposed log houses were stuffed between the logs with clay and moss; mother said so; but I couldn't put the point of my scissors between these logs."

"So they were," said he; "but this is an improved one. Ben means, when he is able, to make this room into two, and have a fireplace in each; and a couple of nice rooms they will make."

"I am glad he didn't do any more. Now, I want to see the kitchen; I care the most about that. This is a splendid one; what nice dressers and drawers! but where is the oven? Why, it's stone; ain't it a beauty; how smooth it is!" said she, putting in her head and shoulders, and feeling all around it with her hands. "I don't see how folks can make such nice things of stone. I wish we had a candle."

She was, if possible, more delighted with the chamber than anything else.

"How high it is!" she said; "what a capital place this would be to spin and weave in! Well, now I've seen the whole."

"No, you haven't;" and here he opened the door in the side of the chimney, and let her look in.

"Why, what in the world is this for?"

"This is a smoke-house; you see it's on one side of the chimney, so that there won't be heat enough go in there to melt the hams or fish. All you have to do, when you want to smoke anything, is to hang it up on these lug-poles, and the common fire you have every day will smoke it. It'll be a nice place for Ben, when he has an ox-yoke, wooden bowl, or shovel to season or toughen. Now I want you to see the cellar."

He pulled from his pocket a horn filled with tinder, and striking a spark into it with a flint and steel, kindled a piece of pitch-wood, and they went down.

"O, my! if here isn't an arch; what a nice place that will be to keep my milk, when I get it."

"Now we've got a light, let's look into the oven."

"I know that oven will bake well," said Sally; "it looks as though it would. Now, I think this is a real nice place, and that Ben has made a good trade; and, if we have our health, we can pay for it well enough. Only think how much we've saved by living in this house, which is good enough for young folks just beginning, and better than many have. Why, it ain't a month since the trees were growing, and now it's all done. Didn't he make a good trade, Uncle Isaac?"

"He made a better one when he got you, you little humming-bird," said Uncle Isaac, who was brim full, and could no longer restrain himself; patting her on the head, "you would suck honey out of a rock."

"I'm much obliged to you, you good old man. I'll tell you what we'll do (that is, when we are able); you shall come over here with Aunt Hannah, and bring all your tools, and we'll part off the front rooms, and have a front entry, ceil up the kitchen, have Uncle Sam to build fireplaces in the front rooms, and Joe Griffin to make fun for us. I'll make you some of those three-cornered biscuit and custard puddings you like so well. In the evenings we'll have a roaring fire; you can tell stories, and we will sit and listen, and knit. Ben says this is the greatest place for gunning that ever was; and you can bring on your float and gun, and you and Uncle Sam can gun to your heart's content. Ain't I building castles in the air?" cried Sally, with another laugh, that made the house ring; "but we must go off, or we shall be caught."

A little breeze had sprung up, and Uncle Isaac putting up a bush for a sail, they landed on the other side without detection.

He said he never wanted to tell anything so much in his life, as he did to tell Ben how much Sally was delighted with the island; but he resolutely kept it to himself.

As it would be difficult getting off in the winter, Ben carried on provisions, hay for a cow, and for oxen that he might get occasionally. He put the hay in a stack out of doors. He bought the hay of Joe Griffin's father, and Joe was to deliver it on the island. Being disappointed in respect to the man who was engaged to help him, he took old Uncle Sam Yelf, as better than nobody. There was a long easterly swell; the scow rolled a good deal, and, the hay hanging over the side and getting wet, she began to fill. At some distance from them Sydney Chase and Sam Hadlock were fishing. "Shall I holler, Mr. Griffin?" said Yelf, who was terribly frightened, and had a tremendous voice.

"Yes."

"What shall I holler?"

"Holler fire."

"Fire! fire! fire!" screamed Yelf.

As their neighbors rowed up, they could not help laughing to see two men up to their waists in water, and one of them crying fire.

"I thought," said the old man, "I'd holler what I could holler the loudest."

CHAPTER XVII.

THEY MARRY, AND GO ON TO THE ISLAND.

THE wedding was at the widow Hadlock's; but Captain Rhines made the infare, as 'twas called,—which was an entertainment given the day after the wedding at the house of the bridegroom. To this were invited all who had aided in building the house, including the girls who prepared the victuals; and a merry time they had of it.

It was very hard for Sally and her mother to part. Since the death of her father, and while the other children were small, Sally had been her mother's great dependence; and, as they came to the edge of the water, the widow lifted up her voice and wept.

Sally, with her eyes full, strove to comfort her mother.

"Well, I ought not to feel so, I know; but it sort o' brings up everything, and tears open all the old wounds. May God bless you! you've been a good child to me in all my trials, and, I doubt not, you'll make a good wife. There's a blessing promised in the Scriptures to those who are dutiful to their parents. Keep the Lord's day, Sally, as you've been taught to do, and seek the one thing needful."

Ben had chosen a sunny, calm morning, that the impressions made upon Sally's mind might be as pleasant as possible, not dreaming that she had already visited the island, and been all over the house. Nevertheless, as he sat down to the oars, his old fears began somewhat to revive; but Providence ordered matters in a much better manner than he could have done, to render Sally's first impressions of the island both pleasant and permanent.

When he left it the last time, knowing that Sally would return with him, he had crammed the great fireplace with dry wood, and pushed under the forestick the top of a dry fir, with the leaves all on, and covered with cones full of balsam. They were well on their way when a black cloud rose suddenly from the north-west, denoting that the wind, which had been south for some days, was about to shift, with a squall.

"We are two thirds over now," said Ben; "we shall be head to the sea, and soon get under the lee of the island; 'tis better to go ahead than to go back."

"I wish we were there now," said Sally to herself, as she thought of that sheltered spot behind the thick woods, that no wind could get through.

"Sit down in the bottom of the canoe, Sally; if the water flies over you, don't move."

When the squall struck, the wind seemed to shriek right out, and in an instant raised a furious sea, drenching them with water from head to foot. Sally uttered not a word, but sat perfectly still, though the cold spray flew over and ran under her, wetting her through and through.

The little boat, managed with consummate skill and strength, rode the sea like an egg-shell. It began to grow smoother as they approached the high woods on the island, when Ben, exerting his strength, drove her through the water, and they were soon at the mouth of the brook, where it was as smooth as a mill-pond. Jumping out, he dragged the canoe from the water, and, taking Sally out, stood her, all dripping, on the beach.

"What a calm place," she exclaimed, "after that dreadful sea! O, you wicked Ben, how could you tell me 'twas such an awful place?"

"You're shaking with the cold; let's go where there's a fire;" and catching her up, he ran into the house with her; then striking fire, he lighted the fir top under the forestick; in an instant the bright flame flashed through the pile of wood, and roared up the chimney, diffusing a cheerful warmth through the room. Ben pulled up the great settle; Sally stretched herself upon it, her wet garments smoking in the heat.

"Isn't this nice?" she said, as, safe from danger, she basked in the warm blaze. "I shall always love this great fireplace after this, as long as I live."

Ben was delighted. He knew by experience the power of strong contrasts, —for the whole life of a seaman is made up of them,—and that nothing could have made the island seem so much like home to Sally, as there finding safety when in danger, and warmth when shivering with cold.

They now went over the house together; and Sally made Ben completely happy by telling him she would have been thankful for a house not half so good. We see in this well-matched and hardy pair the representatives of those who laid broad and deep the foundations of our free institutions, and whose strength was in their homes.

They flung themselves with alacrity upon these hardships, which were to procure for them a heritage of their own,—the product of their own energies, —confident in their own resources, and the protection of that Being whom they had been educated to believe helps those who help themselves.

They were now on an island, in the stormy Atlantic, six miles from the nearest land, which, with the exception of a little strip of grass along the beach, was an unbroken forest.

Here they had commenced married life, in the face of a long, hard winter.

It may seem to many of our readers idle to talk about happiness in relation to people in such circumstances. They, perhaps judging from their own feelings, wonder how they could pass their time.

In the first place, they had health and strength, were not troubled with dyspepsia, and hence did not look at life through green spectacles. They took pride in overcoming obstacles, and feeling that they were equal to the emergency. They had plenty to do from the time they rose in the morning till they went to bed at night; not a moment to brood over and dread difficulties; and a June day was too short for all they found to do in it. Finally, they loved each other, had an object to look forward to, had never known any of those things which are considered by many as necessary to happiness, and thus neither pined after nor missed them.

Sally had plenty of bed-clothes, which she had made herself; also beautiful table-cloths and towels of linen, figured, that she had spun, woven, and bleached; and tow towels, coarse sheets, and table-cloths for every day. One little looking-glass, about six inches by eight in size, graced the wall, with a comb-case, made of pasteboard, hanging below it. They had one really beautiful piece of furniture, which her father had brought from England—a mahogany secretary, with book-cases and drawers, and inlaid with different kinds of wood, contrasting strangely with the rough logs against which it rested. They had chairs with round posts, and bottoms made of ash-splints; mugs, bowls, a tea-pot, and pitchers of earthen ware; and pewter plates, from the largest platter to the smallest dishes and porringers; also an iron skillet. Ben had a shoe-maker's bench, awls and lasts, and quite a good set of carpenter's tools.

Sally now put all the earthen and new pewter ware upon the dressers, which made quite a show.

"I declare, Ben, I've forgotten my candle-moulds, and we've got no light. Here's a lamp, but not a drop of oil or wick in it."

"I'll shoot a seal,—I saw three or four on the White Bull when we came over,—then to-morrow you can try out the blubber."

Ben was better than his word, for before night he shot two.

There was one piece of property that Sally valued more than anything else, because 'twas alive, and there was such a look of home about it.

The widow Hadlock had a line-backed cow, that gave a great mess of milk. Sally had milked her ever since she was large enough to milk; indeed, she milked her that memorable night when Ben and Sam Johnson went blueberrying in the widow's parlor.

They raised a calf from her, which was marked just like the old cow, and Mrs. Hadlock had given it to Sally. The creature, having been brought up with a large stock of cattle, missing her mates, had been very lonesome on the island, and roared and moaned a great deal. As Sally opened the door to throw out some water, the heifer came on the gallop, and, putting her feet on the door-stone, rubbed her nose against Sally's shoulder, and licked her face. The tears came into Sally's eyes in a moment. "You good old soul," said she, putting her arms round her neck,—half a mind to kiss her,—"do you know me, and were you glad to see me? I wish I had an ear of corn to give you."

After this the cow made no more ado, but went to feeding, perfectly contented with the knowledge that her old mistress was present. As night came on, Sally made the discovery that they had no milk-pail; but Ben was equal to the emergency: he cut down a maple, cut a trough in it, drove the cow astride of it, while Sally milked her into this novel pail. That evening Ben dug out a pine log, put a bottom in it, and a bail, then drove two hoops on it, and made a milk-pail.

The next day Sally tried out the seals, while Ben went into the swamp and got some cooper's flags, which he cut into short pieces, for lamp-wicks.

Fowling, for a person in Ben's situation, was not merely a source of pleasure, but of profit, as the feathers sold readily for cash, the bodies were good for food, and could be exchanged at the store for groceries, or with the farmers for wool and flax, which Sally made into cloth.

Ben had a little yellow dog, with white on the end of his tail, that would *play*. Sea-fowl possess a great share of curiosity, which leads them to swim up to anything strange, in order to see what it is. They would often swim in to a squirrel, playing in the bushes at the water's edge, to see what he's about. The gunners take advantage of this trait in their character; they teach a little dog to play with a stone on the beach: he'll roll it along the ground, stand up on his hind legs with it in his fore paws, and when he gets tired of it, his master'll throw him another from his ambush. The birds swim in to see what he is doing, and are killed, and the little dog swims off and brings them ashore. All dogs cannot be taught this, only those who have a genius for it.

Tige Rhines would pick up birds right in the surf, or in the dead of winter, but could never be taught to play; he was too dignified.

It is impossible for one destitute of a taste for fowling to conceive of the intensity which the passion will acquire by indulgence. Ben was so eager for birds, that he would lie on a ledge till Sailor froze his ears and tail. There were a great many minks on the island, whose furs were valuable: these Sailor would track to their holes, when Ben would smoke them out.

The widow Hadlock had brought up her family to cherish a great reverence for the Lord's day. Ben had been trained by his mother in the same way; but, after leaving home, he, like most seafaring men, carried a traveller's conscience, and did many things on that day which would not have met her approval.

One Sabbath morning a whole flock of coots swam into the mouth of the brook to drink; 'twas a superb chance for a shot. Ben, without a moment's hesitation, took down his gun from the hook, and was just going out the door when Sally laid her hand on his arm.

"Ben, where are you going?"

"To shoot those coots; I never saw such a chance for a shot in my life. I shouldn't wonder if I could knock over twenty with this big gun."

"Why, Ben, you must be out of your head; do you know what day 'tis? would you go gunning on the Lord's day?"

"No, I wouldn't *go* a-gunning; but when they come right in under my nose, asking to be shot, I'd shoot them."

"Well, I never would begin by breaking the Lord's day; 'tis not right, and we shall not prosper; if we've not much else, let us, at least, have a clear conscience. What do you think your father and mother would say, if they heard you had fired a gun on the Lord's day?"

"It wouldn't trouble father much; he would do the same himself; but 'twould mother, and I see it does you."

He took his ramrod, and thumped on the side of the house; the coots took to flight in an instant.

"There goes the temptation," said he. "I didn't know before that you was a professor of religion."

"No more I ain't, nor a possessor either; wish I was; but I mean to keep the Lord's day; I'll do that much, any way."

"I know you're right, Sally; but you must make some allowance for a feller who has been so long at sea, and couldn't keep it, if he would, as people can ashore. Suppose a hawk was carrying off a chicken on the Sabbath—wouldn't you let me shoot it?"

"No, I'm sure I wouldn't; but if an eagle was carrying off a baby, I would."

This was the first and only time Ben ever took the gun down on the Sabbath. They made it a day of rest.

They had some good books, and one Sally's mother had given her, which she was very fond of reading, called "Hooks and Eyes for Christian's Breeches." It was a queer title, but a very good book. In those days people did not wear suspenders, but kept their breeches up by buttoning the waistband, or by a belt. Where people were well-formed, and had good hips, they would keep up very well; but when they were all the way of a bigness, or were careless and didn't button their waistbands tight, they would slip down; so some had hooks and eyes to keep them up, and prevent this by hooking them to the waistcoat. Thus this book was designed for those slouching, careless Christians who needed hooks and eyes to their breeches, and were slack in their religious duties.

CHAPTER XVIII.

THE BRIDAL CALL.

PARENTS and friends of the new-married pair had watched with no small anxiety their progress through the squall. During the height of it, they could see the canoe when it rose upon the top of a wave; as it disappeared in a trough of the sea, the widow clasped her hands convulsively, and gave them up for lost.

"They are safe," cried Captain Rhines, drawing a long breath; "they've got under the lee of the island. John, run to the house and get my spy-glass."

With the aid of the glass he saw them land, and Ben carry Sally to the house in his arms.

"She's fainted with fright, poor thing; it's a rough beginning for her," said the widow.

"He only wants to get her to the fire; there's nothing the matter with her but a good soaking."

'Twas now the Indian summer, with calm moonlight nights.

"Wife," said Captain Rhines, "I expect Sally's mother is dying to know how she got on the island that morning. If we don't go now, we shan't be able to go this winter; it'll be too rough by and by. John, run over there, and ask her if she would like to go and see Sally."

"Can I go, too, father?"

"Yes, I want you to help row; so do your chores, tie up the cattle, and bear a hand about it."

Sally had washed her supper dishes, and Ben was pulling off his boots, when the door was opened, and in walked the party. It was a most joyful surprise to the new-married couple.

"Why, mother!" exclaimed Sally, kissing her again and again; "I was thinking the other day whether you would ever venture to come on to this island; and now you're here so soon, and in the fall of the year, too!"

"Indeed, Sally, you know I never lacked for courage, only for strength. You must needs think I had a strong motive."

But, of all the group, none seemed more delighted than John. He stared at the log walls, looked up the chimney, capered round the room with Sailor, and finally getting up in Ben's lap, put both arms round his neck, and fairly cried for joy.

"How should you like to live on here, Johnnie?" said Ben.

"O, shouldn't I like it! you'd better believe."

"I shot two seals the other day, on the White Bull; and within a week I've killed fifty birds, of all kinds."

"Won't you ask father to let me come on and stay a little while, and go gunning? O, I do miss you so!"

"I shouldn't wonder if there were ducks now feeding on the flats; take my gun; she's all loaded."

The moment Sailor saw the gun taken down, he was all ready: so perfectly was he trained, that when it was not desirable he should play, he would lie still till the gun was fired, and then bring in the game.

"How I should like to be on here in the daytime!" said John. "Do you know, Ben, I was never here in all my life before?"

"Why, Sally," said her mother, "how did you get over in that dreadful squall? We were all watching you, and felt so worried! Wasn't you frightened almost to death?"

"No, mother, I wasn't much frightened; but I was terrible cold, and wet all through. I never saw anything look so good, in all my life, as this great fireplace did, for Ben made a roaring fire in it; and I'm just as happy and contented as I can be."

In the midst of this conversation the door opened, and in walked Uncle Isaac.

"It was such a pleasant night," said he, addressing the captain, "I told Hannah we'd take a run down to your house; and when I found you'd come over here, I thought I'd take your gunning float and follow suit."

"Why didn't you bring Hannah with you?" inquired Sally.

"Well, I wanted to; but she ain't much of a water-fowl, and was afraid to come in a tittlish gunning float, and said she'd stay and visit Captain Rhines's girls; but she sends her love to you, and says if she'd known I was coming, she'd sent you over a bag of apples."

"How this does carry a body back!" said the widow; "it don't seem but t'other day since I was living in a log house; and how much I've been through since then!"

They then went all over the house, and down cellar.

"Well, Isaac," said Captain Rhines, "you've done yourself credit in building this house; I knew you would. 'Tisn't much like the house I was born in; that wasn't tighter than a wharf, except while it was stuffed with moss and clay; and some of that was always falling out. I've gone to bed many a night, and waked up in a snow drift, because the wind had blown the clay out, and the snow in; but I thought, when I was coming up from the shore, and saw it standing here in the moonlight, that it was as much like the one father built, after his boys got big enough to be of some help to him, as two peas in a pod: just as many windows, just as high, and with a bark roof; but it ain't much like it other-ways; for the timber wan't hewed—only the bark and knots taken off where it came together; but this is as tight as a churn. And then that fireplace; I wouldn't believed it possible."

"Well," said Uncle Isaac, "I did the best I could; but I think Sam beat the whole of us. I should be glad to swap my fireplace and chimney for that, and give a yoke of oxen to boot."

"Do you know, Isaac, there's nothing carries me back to my boy days like that old chamber? It's the very image of ours; it seems to me as if I was setting there now, on a rainy day, astraddle of a tub, shelling corn on the handle of mother's frying-pan, with my thoughts running all over the world, longing to go to sea, and contriving how I should get father's consent."

A loud mewing was now heard in the corner of the room.

"I declare to man," said the widow, "I've been so taken up with old times, I forgot. See here, Sally,"—opening her basket and taking out a kitten,—"I thought she'd be company for you. You know them speckled chickens, Sally, that the old top-knot hen hatched out."

"Yes, mother."

"Well, the hawks carried off three of 'em; and I meant to brought the rest over to you, but Sam said they wouldn't lay much this winter; you'd have to buy corn, and you'd better have 'em in the spring. But I've brought you over a pillow-case full of flax."

"I," said Mrs. Rhines, "brought you over some wool."

"And I," said Captain Rhines, "a barrel of cider and some vegetables, to go with your coots and salt beef."

"While I," said Uncle Isaac, "am all the one that's come empty-handed; but I know what I'll do; I'll give you a pig, and Ben can get him next time he comes off."

John now came in, bringing five ducks, that he had shot.

"He's just like the rest of us, Ben," said his father: "I believe it runs in the breed of us to shoot."

"Let him come over here, and stay a day or two, and gun with me."

"He's too good a boy,"—patting him fondly on the head;—"I couldn't get along without him."

"That is just the reason," said his mother, "that he ought to be gratified once in a while. It's a great deal better he should be here with Ben, than with some of the boys he goes with; I should feel much easier about him than I do when he's with them in boats, and gunning. I'm always afraid they'll shoot one another, or be drowned."

"Well, it's just as his mother says; I'm at home so little, I don't interfere with her concerns; she's cap'n; I'm only passenger."

"But you're going to be at home all the time now; and I should like to give up my authority."

"By the way, Ben, I've had a letter from Mr. Welch; he says large, handsome masts, bowsprits, and spars are in great demand; that he can find a market in Boston and Salem, in the spring, for all you can send him."

"I'm going to cut small spars directly, father; but I want snow to fall the large ones on, else I shall have to bed them with brush, for fear of breaking them."

"He says that the war in Europe is throwing all the carrying trade into the hands of neutrals; that now we've got our government going, it'll be snapping times; and that while they're all fighting like dogs over a bone, we can run off with the bone; and if I want to try a voyage, he has a vessel for me."

"Well, you're not going," said his wife; "you've been enough, and you've done enough. If Ben could afford to give up going to sea, in the prime of life, for the sake of Sally, I'm sure you can, in your old age, for the sake of Betsey; and you belong to me for the rest of your life."

"Old!" said the captain, dancing over the room; "I don't feel a bit old. I should like a little cash, just to fix up the buildings a little, buy that timber lot that joins the rye field; and then"—with a comical look at his wife—"I should like to do a little more for the minister. I should be so thankful, sometimes, if somebody would come in that could talk about anything else than some old horse, or cow, or sheep that's got the mulligrubs!"

"Father," said John, as they were preparing to go, "why can't I stay now?"

"Because, child, I want you to help me row."

"Let him stay," said Uncle Isaac, who, from instinct, always took the part of the boys; "I'll go over with you."

"But there's my float over here, and I want to go gunning to-morrow."

"We'll take her in tow," said Uncle Isaac.

With mutual good wishes they now separated, leaving John in high glee at the result, with Ben, for a visit.

CHAPTER XIX.

AN UNGRATEFUL BOY.

It may seem very singular to some of our readers, that Captain Rhines, whom we have spoken of as having a strong attachment to the soil, should express a willingness so soon to leave it. But this will not seem at all remarkable to any seafaring man whose eye may chance to glance over our pages.

He had in early years been prevented from gratifying this inclination. On the other hand, his life from boyhood had been spent at sea, in company with seafaring men, and amid excitement and peril. The habits of years are not easily to be overcome; and as age had made no impression upon his iron constitution, after being at home a few months, an almost irresistible longing came over him, at times, to be once more among the very perils he had so congratulated himself upon having escaped, and to hear some talk except about barley and butter.

He also, the moment he came home, began to make improvements—as he said, made things look "ship-shape." But this required money, and he missed the cash he was accustomed to receive at the end of a voyage; besides, a trip to the West Indies seemed to the old sailor as mere recreation, which would enable him to carry out some of his farm produce as a venture, and get his sugar, molasses, coffee, and rum. Had he abandoned the sea at Ben's age, before its habits had ripened into a second nature, it would have been another matter.

John remained on the island a week. On his return he received a warm welcome from Tige, who met him at the shore, and almost wagged his tail off, he was so glad to see him. He had been perfectly miserable without John, for they were inseparable companions. Not knowing how otherwise to express his joy, he began to take up sticks in his mouth, and run about with them.

"Here, old fellow," said John; "if you want something to do, take these birds and carry them to the house, for our dinner."

"John," said his father, "have you had as good a time as you expected?"

"O, father, I never had such a good time in all my life! You know the brook?"

"Yes."

"Well, it's the greatest place for frost-fish you ever did see. The sea-fowl come in there to drink, and there is the best chance to creep to them behind the wood. You never saw such a good dog to play as Sailor is; you throw him a stone, and he'll play half an hour with it. What's Tige been about, father, since I've been gone?"

"Well, when he wan't down on the beach watching for you, barking and whining, he was smelling all round the barn and orchard, and going up in your bedroom: he has rooted the clothes of your bed a dozen times, to see if you was in it; and every night he has slept on your old jacket."

The opinion expressed by John's mother, that 'twas much better he should be on the island than in the company of some of the boys he went with, grew out of the following circumstances:—

During the past summer, a boy by the name of Peter Clash ran away from a Nova Scotia vessel, that came in for a harbor. Old Mr. Smullen had taken him in, out of charity. This boy was eighteen years of age, and belonged in Halifax, where, having the run of the streets and wharves, he learned all kinds of vice. He was of a malicious disposition, and intolerably lazy.

He soon made the acquaintance of all the boys in the neighborhood, but consorted chiefly with Fred Williams, the miller's son, John Pettigrew, Isaac Godsoe, Henry Griffin, and some others.

None of these boys would have been disposed to engage in any mischief beyond mere fun, or that was injurious to any one's person or property, if left to themselves; they also had but little leisure, as, when not at school, they were at work; but Peter, who did very much as he pleased at old Uncle Smullen's, had a great deal of spare time, when he both planned mischief and persuaded the others to aid him in the execution. He had been in the place but a month, when he manifested his mean, cowardly disposition by a trick that he played upon his benefactors.

The old people had fed, clothed, and sheltered him when he had no place to put his head, for which the little labor he performed was by no means an equivalent, as he generally contrived to be out of the way just when his help was needed.

In those days nobody thought of hauling up a year's stock of wood, and having it cut and dried; but they picked it up as they wanted it, and hauled it home on a sled, as wheels were by no means common in those days. The old folks were in the habit of getting on the sled, and riding out in the woods with Peter, helping him load, and then riding back.

Peter had found a large hornet's nest in a heap of beech limbs; so he drives the sled right over it, and stops the cattle; when the enraged insects, who were of the yellow-bellied kind, and the most cruel of stingers, attacked the old people, and stung them terribly, as they were too feeble to get quickly away.

It was thought the old gentleman would never see again. They then turned upon the oxen, who, frantic with fear and agony, ran into the woods, tore the sled in pieces against the trees, and ran into the water, where they would have been drowned but for Joe Bradish and Captain Rhines.

Peter pretended that he didn't know the hornets were there, and the kind old people believed him; but it came out afterwards that he had done it on purpose.

He used also to torment small boys, whenever he could get a good opportunity.

It was the influence of these boys which Mrs. Rhines feared; but she apprehended danger where none existed. Peter, John despised: as to the others, they were too much below him in point of intelligence and force of character to exert any influence over him.

He was now in his fifteenth year, very large of his age, beautifully proportioned, with his father's gray eyes and dark hair; excelled in wrestling, swimming, and all kinds of boys' sports, and bade fair almost to rival Ben in strength. He had an eye that you could look right into, as you can look down into the depths of a clear spring. The whole expression of his face was so manly and frank, it was felt at once to be an index of his character. According to Fred Williams, John Rhines was just as full of principle as he could stick; and the boys never thought of proposing to him any plan which their consciences told them was of doubtful morality. John was less accessible to temptation, for the reason that he loved out of doors, and the stimulus his nature craved was of a healthy character. He delighted in everything that required great physical force and endurance; and we cannot but think that the wrestling, jumping, pulling up, and rough out-door sports of that period, though a man's leg was broken now and then, or somebody killed outright, were infinitely preferable to the effeminate amusements of the present day, which turn boys into coxcombs and men-milliners, and destroy both soul and body. Nothing was more agreeable to him than the pleasure derived from contrasts between great extremes. Those pursuits which promised neither peril nor hardship possessed for him very little attraction.

He loved to fly through the water in a boat, with all the sail she would suffer, while the spray came by bucketfuls on to the side of his neck, and then, rounding a densely-wooded point, run her into a calm, sunny nook, among the green leaves, exchanging the dash of the cold spray and the shrill whistle of the wind for the warm sunshine and the song of birds.

His father used to say he believed that John would pound his finger for the sake of having it feel better when it was done aching; not considering that the boy inherited his own temperament, and that he had manifested the same disposition, when, basking in the warmth of a blazing fire, filled to repletion with sea pie and pudding, he told his wife how much the recollection of his past perils added to his present happiness.

To complete the sum of John's attractions, his voice was naturally modulated to express every shade of feeling; as Uncle Isaac said, "it came from the right place, and went to the right place."

CHAPTER XX.

PETER CLASH AND THE WOLF-TRAP.

Captain Rhines was called to Boston on account of some business with Mr. Welch, and John was kept from school to take care of matters at home.

One pleasant morning, his mother having given him the day, he had made up his mind to go gunning and fishing, taking his dinner with him, Sam Hadlock having agreed to do what was necessary in his absence.

As he was about to set out, Fred Williams came along, with his dinner-pail in his hand, on his way to school.

"Where are you going, John?"

"Frost-fishing and gunning."

"I'll go with you; 'tis too pleasant to go to school."

"I wouldn't play truant, Fred."

"Father won't know it; our girls ain't going to-day; so there's nobody to tell."

"But you'll know it yourself, Fred."

"I don't care."

"If you won't play truant, I'll go some Saturday with you."

"Saturdays father makes me work in the mill; he thinks I don't want to play, as other boys do."

John could not persuade him to go to school; so they started off together. They spent the forenoon in gunning. At noon they made a fire on the rocks, made some clay porridge, then took a sea-fowl and dipped into it, feathers and all, coating it completely with clay; they then dug a hole in the ground, filling it partly with stones, which they made red hot; on these they put the bird, then threw back the loose earth. After a proper time they took it out, and peeled off the clay, which brought the feathers and skin with it, leaving the carcass clean and well cooked.

John had brought pepper, salt, and butter, and they had plenty of bread and meat in their dinner-pails. Tige wouldn't touch the bird; so they gave him the meat.

"How good this is!" said Fred, with the wing of a sheldrake in his mouth; "how glad I am I didn't go to school!"

John made no reply, for his mouth was full; neither did he approve of playing truant. They now went to Uncle Isaac's brook, fishing. The frost-fish swim up into the mouth of little brooks, where the water is only about two or three inches deep, and are very slow in their movements in cool weather. The boys caught them by fastening a cod-hook to a stick, three or four feet long, and hauling them out. They set out on their return in good season, that Fred might get home at the proper time, and escape detection.

As they came to the landing, John jumped out to haul the boat ashore, while Fred pushed with an oar; the boat, striking a rock, stopped so suddenly, that he fell down into the bottom of her, and stuck one of the hooks into his thigh. The remorseless steel buried itself in the flesh beyond the barb. There was the miserable boy, with both hands behind him, holding himself up, afraid either to get up or sit down, as he could not move an inch without taking with him the great stick to which the hook was fastened. John, reaching carefully under him, cut the string which fastened it to the hook, letting it fall off.

Fred now prostrated himself on the beach, while John proceeded to examine; he pulled a little.

"O-w-w! you hurt me!"

"It's over the barb; I can't pull it out without almost killing you."

"My father'll kill me quite, if he finds out I've played truant; father's awful when he rises. O, I wish I'd gone to school."

"I should think you would."

"It must come out somehow; can't you *cut* it out?"

"I'll try; but it'll hurt."

"I can't help it; but be as easy as you can."

John had been shelling clams with his knife the day before, and that forenoon he'd used it as a screw-driver, to tighten the flint in his gun; but he whet it on the sole of his boot, and began to cut.

"O, dear! what shall I do? Boo-oo! cut away, John! I shall die! I shall die! I wish I'd gone to school! Murder! murder!! murder!!!"

"Fred," cried John, flinging away the knife, his eyes filling with tears, "I can't bear to hurt you so."

"Father'll hurt me worse; he'll rip it right out, and lick me into the bargain."

"There's a file in the canoe, they have to sharpen hooks; perhaps I can file it off."

"Do, John; do."

Just as the voices of the children were heard going home from school, John succeeded in filing it off. Fred jumped up, his mouth full of gravel, where he had bitten the beach in his agony, and ran home. He didn't sleep much that night. The sawing of the flesh with a dull knife produced irritation, and by morning it began to fester. It hurt him to walk, it hurt him to move, and it hurt him to sit still. All day long he sat on the edge of his seat, and didn't go out at recess to play. When he got home, he found his cousin John Ryan had come to spend the night. As he was a general favorite, the children all wanted him to sit next them at the table. They were all standing up around the table, wrangling about it, when the miller, who had a grist to grind before dark, and was in a hurry for his supper, lost all patience.

"Down with you—will you, somewhere?" cried he to Fred; "you're big enough to behave," and pushed him slap down into a chair.

"O!" screamed Fred, jumping upright, bursting into tears, and clapping both hands to the aggrieved part.

It all came out now; but in consideration of what he had suffered, and had yet to undergo, he escaped a whipping. His mother bound some of the marrow of a hog's jaw on the wound, and, after a while, the hook came out.

Fred promised John Rhines solemnly that he not only would never play truant again, but in all respects try to become a better boy; yet the wound was scarcely healed before he was again engaged in mischief.

Captain Rhines had a fish-flake on the beach, just above high-water mark. Uncle Isaac had been making fish on it, and they were nearly cured.

He cherished a bitter antipathy to the Tories, and, like all the people on the sea-coast of Maine, was inclined to dislike the inhabitants of Nova Scotia, among whom they sought refuge after they were driven from the colonies. This prejudice extended itself to Peter Clash, and was greatly strengthened by his treatment of his benefactors; he therefore never treated him with the cordiality he did the other boys. This Pete highly resented. He persuaded Fred, Jack Pettigrew, Ike Godsoe, and some others, to go with him in the evening, take the fish from the flakes, and throw them on the beach. It was a very difficult matter to persuade the boys to do this, for they all loved and respected Uncle Isaac; besides, he was not a person to be trifled with. After going once, all, except Fred, Jack, and Ike, refused to go again; and after Pete and his satellites had gone, Henry Griffin and the others went back and replaced the fish. Pete, with his crew, continued the sport, and enjoyed a malicious pleasure, as, hid in the bushes, they saw him picking up the fish, many of which, getting in the tide's way, were spoiled.

PETER CLASH AND THE WOLF TRAP. Page 207.

Uncle Isaac set a wolf-trap beside the flake, covering it in the sand, and hid himself among the bushes. The boys manifested a great deal of caution, pretending they had merely come down to fling stones into the water. The conduct of Uncle Isaac, who continued quietly to pick up the fish, without saying a word, made them suspicious; they thought there must be something "under that heap of meal." By and by they began to edge up towards the flake, often stopping to listen. At last Pete went up to the fish; walking along the edge of the flake, he threw off the fish as he went, crying, "There's nobody here; why don't you come on, you cowards." The words were scarcely out of his mouth, when snap went the great iron jaws of the trap, and up jumped Uncle Isaac from the bushes. Pete roared with agony. Well he might; the trap would have cut off his leg, or crushed it to pomace, if Uncle Isaac had not tied down one of the springs, thus diminishing its force. His captor uttered never a word; but catching him up, trap and all, walked right into the water.

"O! Mr. Murch, I'll never do so again! What be you going to do to me?"

"Drown you, you spawn of a Tory; your hide isn't worth taking off."

Pete poured forth agonizing entreaties for mercy, and made the most solemn promises of amendment, if his life could be spared.

"You're a rotten egg; you're spilin' all our boys, you varmint," said Uncle Isaac, chucking him right into the water, head and ears.

"Murder! murder!" screamed Pete, the moment he got his head out.

"Will you clear out in the spring, in the first fisherman that comes along, and go where you come from?"

Pete called God to witness that he would.

"You can do as you like; but if you don't, I'll be the death of you. I calculate," said Uncle Isaac, as he picked up his fish, "he'll keep his word this time; he'll have about as much as he can do to take care of that leg this winter."

John Rhines, being lonesome, after Ben went on to the island, had kept company to some extent with these boys; but it was very much like trying to mix oil and water; they played together occasionally, but there was no fusion. When he heard of the last-mentioned occurrence, he said to his mother,—

"I won't be seen with those boys any more. O, mother, I do wish I had somebody to love besides Tige."

"Why, John Rhines, where are your parents, your sisters, and all your friends?"

"You know what I mean; some boy of my age, that I could love clear through; that you, and father, and Ben could love, and love to have me with; and, when he come to our house, you'd give him a piece of cake, and wouldn't look so, as you do when Fred comes. I mean somebody that wasn't like these boys, either stupid or wicked."

The boy's heart, overflowing with the impulses of youth, longed for a kindred spirit of his own age.

CHAPTER XXI.

WHY THE BOYS LIKED UNCLE ISAAC.

It has been very evident, during the progress of this story, that the young men were very much attached to Uncle Isaac; yet the boys were not a whit the less so; the reasons of which will appear as we proceed.

In the first place, he retained in his feelings all the freshness and exuberance of his youth; they knew that he liked them; and it is strange how this unwritten, unspoken language of the heart is generally felt and understood.

In the next place, he was never known to divulge a secret, and was the depositary of half the love affairs of the young people in the neighborhood; indeed, the boys often confided to him their intended pranks. If mere fun was the object of them, he permitted them to take their course, but, if they were of a malicious nature, would induce them to give them up, by proposing something else,—generally a tramp with him in the woods, or on the water, the seductions of which no boy was able to resist. It was well it was thus, for he knew infinitely better how to manage them than half their parents. It has been well said, that man must look up in order to worship; 'tis just so with boys. A timid, effeminate man can have no influence over a mess of boys; and if you have any doubt on this point, just read the names on the boys' sleds and boats.

When, in the winter, he happened to ride by the school-house, just as school was out, a curious scene presented itself. Children, in those days, were taught to make their manners; but when Uncle Isaac came along, they first made a bow, or dropped a courtesy, just to manifest respect; and then boys and girls would pile into the sleigh, and hang around his neck, till he was well nigh smothered. The old horse would lay back his ears, and look around, as though distrusting his ability to draw the unwonted load; while the schoolmaster, looking out of the window, attracted by the noise, and amused to see the little ones searching his pockets for apples, would forget to notice when the minute-glass had run out.

There was another thing which imparted to his society a wonderful fascination for the boys, which we can in no other way explain so well as by relating a conversation between little Bobby Smullen and his grandfather. The boy was at play before the door, as Uncle Isaac returned from Sam Elwell's, after picking Yelf out of the ditch. He endeavored, with all his might, to entice him to go in, as he wanted to listen, while he talked over old times with his grandparent; but Uncle Isaac was in a hurry, and, patting his head, went on.

Bobby, who was a bright, observing little chap, looked after him till he was out of sight. Going into the house, he said, "Grandsir, what makes Uncle Isaac walk so?"

"Walk how?"

"Why, you know how; he don't walk like other folks."

"The child means," said his grandmother, "because he toes in."

"That's because he's an Indian, Bobby."

"Why, Jonathan, ain't you ashamed of yourself? he's no more of an Indian than you are. I knew his father and mother well; old Mr. Murch and his wife were the best of people."

"Well, the Indians brought him up, anyhow. I don't jestly know the rights of it; but they carried him off, with some others of his people, when he was a boy; part of them they tomahawked, and part they roasted alive; but one of the chiefs took him, and brought him up. He lived with them years and years, learnt their language and their ways, and was as good an Indian as the best of them. I've heard him say, he thought their kind of life was happier than ours; he never will get that wild nature out of him. When the Penobscots come here in the summer, and camp on his point, he'll carry them beef, pork, potatoes, and milk, and says they have as good right here as he has, and better, too. He'll give them anything except rum; he says that wasn't made for an Indian, because it makes him crazy."

"Don't it make white people crazy, too, grandsir?"

"Hush, child; you put me out, and you don't know what you're talking about. For all he's such a desperate working cretur, he'll go down right in haying time, and set on a log, and talk with them, and seems just as uneasy all the time they're about as John Godsoe's geese."

"What about John Godsoe's geese?"

"Nothing, child."

"Yes, there is; I know there is; do tell your little boy, grandsir."

"Why, John's got some wild geese that can't fly, because one joint of their wings is cut off. They go in the pasture with the other geese as peaceable as can be; but in the spring, when the wild ones are flying over and konking, they'll flap their old stubs of wings, and holler, and be as uneasy; that's jest the way Isaac's took when the Indians are round. I sometimes think he'd go off with them, if he could get his family to go."

The horrors of Indian massacre were still fresh in the recollections of older people. Smullen's first wife and old Mr. Yelf's father were both killed by the Indians; and there was nothing more attractive to the youth of that day. No marvel, then, that a romantic interest mingled in the minds of the boys with the affection they entertained for Uncle Isaac.

It is frequently said, one boy is better than two boys, and that three is just no boy at all; but half a dozen of them would work all day for dear life, with Uncle Isaac, encouraged by the promise, always kept, of going on a tramp with him when the job was over. Boys don't like to go gunning, and come home empty-handed. When they went with him, they always brought home game with them; for if they couldn't shoot anything, he could. These attractions enabled him to exert a great influence over them, which he improved to the noblest ends, and made impressions that were never eradicated. He was neither in his own opinion, nor by profession, a religious man; but the teachings of a pious mother had laid deep in his young heart the foundation of faith and love. When torn from her by the savages, in the solitude of mighty forests, he had pored and prayed over them, till they ripened into a heartfelt love for Him "who causeth the grass to grow for cattle, and herb for the service of man."

His teachings were therefore of such a nature, that while divested of the stiffness generally connected with all attempts at advice or instruction, they deepened every good impression, and stirred the young heart to the quick.

A most silly and hurtful notion, often entertained by young people in respect to religion, is, that it has a tendency to make people narrow-minded, or, as they phrase it, meeching. Such a feeling was effectually repressed, as they listened to ideas of that nature from one who hesitated not to grapple with the fiercest beasts of the forest, and bore on his person the scars of many wounds. His influence over them was very much increased, for the reason that he seemed anxious to make them happy in this world, as well as the other; inculcated with great earnestness those principles which lie at the bottom of thrift, competence, and the well-being of society.

Religious discourse from their parents, the catechising of the minister, advice in respect to their conduct in life, might be quite dry and uninteresting; but with what power to attract and move were the same ideas invested, as they fell from the lips of the hunter and warrior, on a wild sea-beach, amid the roar of breakers; in some sunny nook of the hills, with the rifle across his knees, made juicy and attractive by his graphic language; not thrust upon them against the stomach of their sense, but, like the teachings of the great Parent of nature, in harmony with bursting buds, the springing grass, shading into a deeper green, or mingling in their ear with the brook's low murmur, and the music of summer winds among the foliage,—thus imperceptibly, as the increase of their strengthening sinews, growing up with, and moulding the very habit of their thoughts!

There had been no adverse element to disturb these pleasant and profitable relations, till Peter Clash came into the neighborhood. Nothing but the entire conviction of the uselessness of all efforts to reclaim him, and a knowledge of the injury his influence and example was doing to the other boys, caused Uncle Isaac to treat him with such severity, and made him resolve to drive him out of the place.

"I wouldn't be so mean," said he, "as to throw my weeds into other people's gardens; but when they throw their weeds into mine, I'll fling them back again: he shan't take root and go to seed here; we've weeds enough of our own."

The first leisure day John had, after his father's return, he took his hoe, and going directly to the field where he knew Uncle Isaac was digging potatoes, went to work with him.

"I don't mean to play any more with Pete, and that set; I mean to play with you, Uncle Isaac."

"I should like to have a playmate first rate; I've been pretty much alone of late."

"Will you go gunning with me in your float, after we get these potatoes dug?"

"Yes."

"Won't you tell me an Indian story now?"

"I can't talk and work too; but I'll tell you one to-night, after we've done work, and when we go gunning, and are waiting for birds. Work when you work, and play when you play; that's my fashion."

When the time arrived, John reminded Uncle Isaac of his promise.

"Well, John, where do you want to go? into the woods, or after sea-fowl?"

"I'll tell you what I want to do, above all things; but perhaps you wouldn't; I want you to learn me to shoot flying. I can shoot very well now at a dead mark; but I never, in all my life, shot anything flying."

"You'll never be much of a gunner till you can, because there's ten chances to shoot flying or running game where there is one to shoot that which is still.

Take a fox, for instance; 'tain't one time to a hundred you can shoot one, except on the clean jump, going twelve or fifteen foot at a leap, and looking just like a little streak. All these sea-fowl fly out of the bays every night. Now, there's a place between Smutty Nose and the Sow and Pigs, not more than half a gun-shot in width, which they fly through about sunrise, when they come into the bay. I've gone there before sunrise, with three guns, and killed over a hundred; been back by the middle of the forenoon, got my breakfast, and, by working a little later, done a good day's work. What d'ye think of that, Johnny?"

"O!" cried John, his eyes flashing, "I shouldn't want to live any longer, if I could do that."

"There's a good many other places where they fly through; for it's the nature of them to follow the land. They used to fly through between Elm Island and the outer ledges, but I expect Ben has pretty much put an end to that; besides, if you have two guns, or a double barrel, it gives you two chances—you can fire at them in the water, and when they rise give it to them again."

"I know it; I've seen you and Ben shoot wild geese when they were flying over. Ben burnt mother awfully with a wild goose."

"How could that be?"

"Well, mother was frying fish in the Dutch oven; Ben fired into a flock that was flying over the house, and down came an old gander, right down chimney, and flung the fat all over her face."

"Well, John, as to the learning, you must forelay for them; when they're coming towards you, swing your gun as they fly, and aim jest before their bill, and then they'll fly right into the shot. The best bird for a boy to practise on is a fish-hawk, because they are a large mark, and fly steady, but they are all gone south now; but a coot will do very well. You must shoot, and shoot, and practise till you get it; and jest as you begin to think you never can get it, 'twill come. You better take my gun; it goes quicker than yours. I'll manage the boat; you can fire, and I'll watch you and tell you."

On their way home they fell into conversation about the other boys.

"I don't think," said John, "that Fred is a bad-hearted boy; we've always played together, and he was a good boy till Pete came here. I believe all of them would do well enough, if 'twasn't for him, and would never do any real mean mischief of their own heads; they like fun, and so do I, and should be as full of mischief as any of them, if I didn't like gunning so much better, which takes up all my spare time."

"That Pete is too rotten to nail to. As for Fred, there's more foundation to him; he's had a better bringing up; he's like the fish that take the color of the bottom they feed on; he falls in with the company he keeps, and can't stand on his own legs."

"I don't believe I should have been one whit better than Fred, if I had been brought up as he has. I've known Fred to do a real good day's work, and his father and mother never take the least notice of it; now, big boy as I am, there's nothing pleases me so much as to have father come and see what I've done, and praise me for it; then his father always sets his bounds, and tells him he may go to such a tree or rock; of course he wants to go over; he'd be a fool if he didn't. I've gone over there sometimes, all dressed up, to play with him, and his father would keep him to work, when Fred knew, and I knew, that the work might be just as well done the next day. I tell you, that makes a boy feel ugly. Now, just look at my father; I've known him, when boys came over here to play with me, to let me off, and work till after dark himself. Think I didn't put in the next day, and watch for chances to make it up? and do you think I'll ever forget it, as long as I live? 'Tisn't every boy, Uncle Isaac, that's got as good father and mother as I have."

"You never spoke a truer word than that, John."

"I don't believe a boy can love a man, just because he's his father, if he treats him just like a dog."

"Don't you think, then, instead of leaving Fred altogether, it would be better to ask him to go with you and me sometimes?"

"I think we should have a great deal better time without him."

"Perhaps so; but we ought to be willing sometimes to displease ourselves, for the sake of benefiting others. A boy or man, who never thinks of anybody's comfort or happiness but his own, is a pretty mean sort of an affair, and ought not to be allowed round. There's Pete; he's no credit to his Maker, and only a plague to the neighborhood, and swears awful; yet God feeds and clothes him."

"No, he don't, Uncle Isaac; because Mrs. Smullen makes the cloth, and makes the clothes, too."

"If she does, the Lord gives her the stock, and wit, and strength to manufacture it. You allow yourself there's some good in Fred; and I say it's no part of a man, when a poor fellow's on his hands and knees, trying to get up, to jump on him."

"But you don't understand. It isn't just for the sake of going gunning, and hearing the Indian stories, that I like so well to go with you; but I like to hear you talk about good things, and tell me how I can make a man of myself. Fred wouldn't care a straw for such things."

"How can that ever be known, till it's tried? According to your tell, he's never had much of such treatment."

"That is very true."

"You're very sorry he's a bad boy; wish he was better; but are not willing to forego your own pleasure for the sake of getting him into better company, and giving him an opportunity to rally. We've spent all this day, and have patiently managed the boat, that you might learn to shoot flying, and you've made out to kill two birds; whereas, if I'd taken the gun, made you manage the boat, or gone without you, I might have killed twenty, and been home at dinner-time."

"I'm ashamed of myself, Uncle Isaac; I won't be so mean and selfish any more."

"Well, Pete'll have enough to do to take care of his legs this winter, and I think he'll go off in the spring. Speak kindly to Fred, and keep hold of him; and when the warm weather comes, we'll take him with us, and try to save him."

CHAPTER XXII.

BEN'S NOVEL SHIP.

It was now early winter, and the proper time to work in the woods.

"Do you think," said Ben to Uncle Isaac, "I'd better hire Joe?"

"He asks great wages, but he's the cheapest man you can hire, for all that. I've seen a man fall spars, so that they all had to be hauled out top foremost; it was like twitching a cat by the tail. Most men will break more or less masts, falling them, and soon throw away all their wages; but though Joe seems to be such a great heedless creature, there's nothing pertains to falling, hauling, or rafting timber, that he don't know; he can also shave shingles and rive staves, and will be just as profitable in stormy weather as at any other time."

The next morning, as Ben and Joe were grinding their axes to attack the forest, they were very much surprised by a visit from Uncle Isaac.

"I felt," said he, "as though I must look upon Elm Island once more, before the axe and firebrand went into it, and while it was as God made it. Perhaps it's owing to my Indian bringing up, but I hate to see the forest fall; and when I have to go fifty miles to shoot a deer or a bear, the relish will be all taken out of life for me."

"I feel very much as you do," said Ben; "I know I shall spoil its beauty, but I see no other way to pay for it."

"I'm not so sure of that; there's no doubt but Congress, by and by, will give a bounty to fishermen; fishing is going to come up. Mr. Welch don't want his money any more than a cat wants two tails; he told you to take your own time, and I'd take my time. I believe you can pay for this island by clearing only what you need for pasture and tillage. That will make quite a hole in your debt, and the rest you can pull out of the water."

"But I don't want to be a fisherman; I detest it; work all summer, and eat it all up in the winter; so much broken time, when it's so windy you can't fish, and can't do anything else, for fear it will come good weather, and you will have to leave it."

"That's the right kind of talk; I like to hear you talk so; but you can fish till the land is yours—can't you? All the time you are fishing, the timber will be growing, and then you can farm it to your heart's content; farming is going to be a first-rate business, too. People round here are all stark mad about lumbering and fishing; they will touch anything but a hoe, and think barley ain't worth thanking God for. Since the peace, the country is full of foreign goods, and they are ready to strip the land to get money to buy them. Nothing but French calico, silks, and satins, and all such boughten stuffs, will do for 'my ladyship' now. If people are going to work in the woods all winter, and drive the river and work in the mills all summer, I should like to know where the corn, hay, pork, and beef, to feed all these people that grow nothing, is to come from. I wonder if the people that stay at home and raise it won't get a round price for it."

"I've thought of that," said Ben. "I know that a great many fishermen come here for supplies, must have them, and no time to run after them, and will give whatever the men ask that bring them alongside."

"There's another thing; this timber will be worth more every year it stands, because it will be growing scarce."

"O, Uncle Isaac, this is a great country; it won't be till you and I, and our grandchildren, if we have any, are dead and gone."

"That's true; and it ain't true there's no end to the timber in the country; but the timber that is directly on the shore, where a vessel can go right to it, is growing scarce, more especially these big masts. The king's commissioners scoured the sea-coast pretty well before the war; and masts and spars on an island like this, with a good harbor, where they can be got to the ship's tackles with little expense, will, in a few years, bear a great price; for if timber is plenty, labor is not. Thank God, every one has enough to do; and it costs, I can tell you, to bring timber down a river thirty miles, to what it does to roll it off the bank, as you can here."

"I see you are right; for I'm sure I don't know of another island that is timbered like this. Others have all been cut, and burnt over by the fishermen setting fires in the summer; about half the timber on the islands is burnt up by mere carelessness."

"You wouldn't like to lose this brook—would you?"

"Lose the brook! I'd as soon lose the island; it would not be worth much without the brook."

"Well, just as sure as you clear the middle ridge, and the north-east end of the island where the springs are that feed it, and let the sun and wind in on the land, you'll dry the brook."

"Do you think so?"

"I don't *think* so—I *know* so. There's a brook runs through my field. Long since I can remember it used to carry a saw-mill; but my father and I cleared the land, and the people at the source of it cleared theirs, and now it's dry all summer, and but a little water in it early in the spring and late in the fall."

"I'm glad you told me this; you know I'm a sailor, and don't know much about such matters. I hope you'll never be mealy-mouthed, but speak just as you think."

"I'm an ignorant man, and have never been to school, and over the world, as you have; but I know about these sort of things, because I've either tried 'em, or seen other people try them; it's jest my experience."

When he had thus spoken he prepared to depart.

"Do stay to dinner, Uncle Isaac," said Sally.

"It's impossible; I ought to be at home this very minute; but I couldn't help coming over here and freeing my mind;" and, dropping his oars into the water, he was in a moment round the eastern point.

This conversation made a deep impression upon Ben; he looked upon the island not merely as offering advantages for a living, but he loved it. All his ideas of beauty and sublimity were ingrafted upon these woods and shores; from boyhood he had been accustomed to go there with his father. Often, in the lonely hours of the middle watch on the ocean, had memory painted the green foliage of the birches drooping over the high ledge.

In many a black night of tempest, as he stood amid the pouring rain and flashing lightning, did his thoughts revert to that tranquil cove, reflecting from its bosom the overhanging rocks and trees, while the sunlight of a summer's morning was glancing on the glossy breasts of the sea-ducks sporting in its calm waters.

Standing upon the beach where he had parted with his friend, he looked over the scene, and pictured to himself the middle ridge, shorn of its green coronal of majestic forest, covered with blackened stumps and the charred ruins of mighty trees. The interlacing network of tree-roots, ferns, and mosses of a thousand hues, that now adorned the rocks, burnt off, leaving them white and barren, and the bare bones of the soil sticking out. No shelter for fruit trees or crops, man or beast, and the supply of water greatly diminished; the sweet music of the brook hushed, and the multitudes of hawks and herons, who, notwithstanding their harsh notes, could ill be spared, banished forever, and the island left a shelterless rock in the ocean for the cold sea winds to whistle over.

He found that Sally shared his feelings in the fullest extent, and together they resolved to submit to any privations, and make every possible effort in order to save, at least, a good part of the forest.

The axes now went merrily from daylight till dark. They made a workshop of the front part of the house, and in stormy days made staves and shingles, as there were many trees, which, after they were cut, proved to have a hollow in the butt, or were "konkus," and, though not suitable for spars, made good shingles. Sometimes an oak was in the way of a road, which, cut, made staves.

Ben, while privateering, had taken from a prize some fine rifles; two of these he sold, and bought a large yoke of oxen, and hiring four more, he began to haul his spars to the beach. As the distance was short, and the ground in general descending, he did not wait for snow, but hauled the smallest spars on the bare ground, leaving the large masts and bowsprits till the snow came. This was not so difficult as it might appear; for it is very different hauling in the woods from doing the same thing on a road. The ground was in most places covered with a network of roots, strewn with leaves and frozen, and the sled slipped over these quite easily; besides, wherever there was a hard spot, or a hollow, they cut small trees, peeled the bark off, and put them along the road for the sled to slip over, and thus, though they could not move the largest sticks in this way, they got along as fast with the others as though there was snow; for if they hauled smaller loads, having no snow to wade through, and no road to break, they went the oftener. Even when the snow came, his team was light to haul some of the biggest masts; but they made calculations take the place of strength, put rollers under the sticks, and helped the cattle with a tackle.

Thus they spent the winter. As the spring came on, how he longed to plough up the clear spot along the beach, to plant a few peas and potatoes, or set out a currant bush or two in the warm sunny ground, under the high ledge, that every time he passed it seemed to say, "Do plant me, Ben."

How much more difficult it was to let the wild geese alone, that were flying in vast flocks over his head! It made him half crazy to hear the guns of Uncle Isaac, John, and his father, who were letting into them right and left, as they went, bang, bang.

It was not like the gunning nowadays, when a great lazy fellow goes all day to shoot a sandpiper or a sparrow; but there was profit as well as sport in it. Nevertheless, he manfully resisted temptation, and plied the axe.

"I'll not live another spring without a gunning float," said he to Joe, and dismissed the matter from his thoughts.

"What fools we are!" said Joe; "we've not had a drink of sap yet." As he spoke, he struck his axe with an upward blow into the body of a rock maple, and stuck a chip in the gash; he then cut down a small hemlock, took off a length, and from it made a trough. The sap ran down the chip into the trough, and in a few hours they had enough to drink.

"How good that looks!" said Joe, as he got down on his hands and knees, and looked into the luscious liquid, as clear as crystal; "and it don't taste bad, neither."

The first thing Joe did the next morning was to visit the trough, expecting to find it full; but it was entirely empty.

"It was half full when I left it, and it must have run fast; what a fool I was I didn't drink it all up! I know who's got it," cried he, as he noticed on a little patch of snow some tracks, that looked not unlike those made by the bare feet of little children, for they had been enlarged by the thawing of the snow; "they are that coon's wife and children, that we killed when we were hewing timber. They will be nice neighbors, Ben, when you come to plant corn here."

"I don't care if they do eat a little corn; I want all the neighbors I can get. It will be first rate to know just where to go and get a coon when you want one. I shall be as well to do as the grand folks in England, and have my own game preserve; besides, if they get troublesome, I can kill them all with Sailor in a week, on a place no larger than this."

There was no vessel in that vicinity larger than a fisherman's, or a wood coaster. It required a vessel of larger size to carry such spars, and to have hired one from a distance would have eaten up a great part of their value. Determined at any risk to save a great part of the forest, he devised and executed a most audacious plan, that he might realize every dollar from the sale of his spars, by avoiding the great expense of transportation.

With a cool daring and skill, perfectly characteristic, he rolled his masts and spars on to the beach, where, by the help of the tide, he could handle them as he pleased, and built them somewhat into the shape of a vessel, securing the whole firmly together with cross-ties and treenails. He then made a large oar to steer with, which no one but himself could lift, that worked in a port, so that it could not slip out and float up. He then put a large timber across the stern, with deep notches cut in it, to hold the oar in whatever direction he placed it, in order that he might be able to leave it, and go to other parts of the raft to attend to other matters. A mast had been already built in when the raft was made; he bought an old mainsail that belonged to John Strout, made for the Perseverance, and put a cable, anchor, and boat-compass on board.

"I must have a chance to make a cup of tea," said Ben; "for I shall be up nights, as there's only one in a watch."

They placed a large flat stone in the midst of the raft to build the fire on, and then made a fireplace with stones laid in clay, to prevent the wind from blowing the fire away from the kettle. Two crotches were then placed each side of the fireplace, and a pole put across to hang the tea-kettle on. Wood and water were now put on board; some dry eel-grass to lie down on; staves, shingles; and feathers, the results of gunning at odd times; and the preparations for the voyage were complete.

"Ben," said his wife, "Joe says you are going to Boston on that thing alone?"

"I'm going to set out, Sally. I can tell you better when I come back, whether I get there or not."

"Suppose you should get blown off to sea, and never be heard from again."

"Suppose, what is more likely, I shouldn't."

"Suppose the raft should come to pieces."

"Suppose it should stay together. We never shall save the woods, and the beach, and all the pretty things, if it costs half the spars are worth to get them to market."

"Better lose the island than your life; what if there should come a big sea, and wash you overboard?"

"What, if when the angels were taking Elijah to heaven, they had let him drop?"

Perceiving he had fully made up his mind, she said no more, but quietly set about preparing his food for the voyage. This was put under the canoe, which was turned bottom up on the raft, and lashed.

There were but four pieces of rope on the whole raft, for rope was high in those days: these were the cable, the canoe's painter, and the sheet and halyards of the sail.

The logs were lashed with withes, as also the canoe, water, and other things. These withes were of enormous strength, though stiff and hard to handle; for many of them were as thick as a man's wrist, which Ben twisted as though they had been willow switches.

Ben had not mentioned his plan to any one out of his own house, but, when the wind came in strong from the north-east, set sail just as the sun came up.

The first proceeding of John Rhines at this time of year, when he got out of bed, was to look out of his window, to see if there were any wild geese round that were anxious to be shot, that he might give the alarm to his father. No sooner did he espy the novel craft come out from the harbor, and proceed to sea, than going down stairs three steps at a time, he shouted, "Father! father! see what this is!"

"It is a raft, that has come down from the head of the bay, and is going over to Indian Creek Mill."

"But it came from Elm Island; I saw it."

"You thought it did; but it came down by it, and appeared to you to come from it."

"No, father; it came right out of the harbor, for I saw it with my own eyes."

"Get the glass, John; that will tell the story." Resting the glass on the fence, he looked long and carefully. At length he said, "John, that's your brother Ben on that raft. He's got half an acre of spars, I verily believe—all they have cut this winter; well, he's one of the kind to make a spoon or spoil a horn—always was."

"But where's he going to?"

"Boston, I expect; he's steering that way, and is making first-rate headway, too."

Forgetting all about his breakfast, John ran to Uncle Isaac's, while Captain Rhines went in to tell the news to his wife.

"Ben's going to Boston on a raft!" he shouted; "O, come quick, or he'll be out of sight!"

They watched him from the hill, and then from the garret window, till he disappeared from view.

"If the wind should come in fresh at north-west," said Uncle Isaac, "no power on earth could prevent his going to sea, and that would be the end of him;" but, noticing the look of anxiety upon John's face, he said, "Come in and take breakfast with us, and then we'll see what your father thinks about it."

"Don't you think Ben's running a great risk?" asked Uncle Isaac of Captain Rhines.

Now, Captain Rhines had never done much else, except to run risks, and therefore was not particularly sensitive on that score.

"It's a risk, that's certain; but then it's a risk that's well worth the running, to get such a tremendous raft of spars as that to market, as you may say, for nothing. The wind often holds easterly, this time of year, a fortnight; it's our trade-wind; he is going every bit of four knots. I'll risk Ben; he's one of the kind that always come on their feet. There's not another man in the world that looks as bad as he does, that would have got Sally Hadlock. Nobody else could have got Elm Island from Father Welch. I have been trying to buy it of him these twenty years; but he said it was his father's before him, and he wouldn't sell it, for he didn't want to see it stripped; and he knew I would cut the timber off the first thing. No, I'll risk Ben. Did I ever tell you what a Yankee trick he served a British man-of-war, when he was captain of a privateer?"

"No; what was it? I didn't know he ever was captain."

"Well, he never was, only in this way. Their captain was killed in action with an armed merchantman; Ben, being lieutenant, took charge, and acted as captain the rest of the cruise. You see, they were cruising off the coast, to try and cut off some of the English supply vessels, that were bringing provisions and ammunition to their armies, for our folks were mighty short of powder, and everything else, for the matter of that. They were lying by in a thick fog —not a breath of wind—couldn't see your hand before you; and when the fog lifted at sunrise, they were right under the guns of a fifty-gun ship, that was off there looking out for the expected transports. No squeak for them. What does Ben do but strip off his clothes, get into his berth, and make the doctor bind his right leg and arm all up with splinters and bandages, as though they were broken, then bleed him, and put the blood over the wound, as though it had been done by a shot! John Strout was second mate; so he became first mate, or first lieutenant, when Ben took charge; you know he and Ben are like knife and fork—always together. The man-of-war put a prize captain and crew on board, and put Ben's crew in irons, and ordered her into New York. They took him out of his berth, and put him between decks with his men, which was just what he wanted, though he groaned and took on terribly when they were moving him, it hurt him so; and the doctor said 'twas real barbarity to move a patient in his condition.

"The English in time of war were always short of seamen,—more so now than ever,—as they were fighting with us and France both; they had but few men to spare for a prize crew; they took out part of Ben's crew, and put the rest in irons; made a captain of an old quartermaster, with two midshipmen for lieutenants; gave them about a dozen seamen, and three or four petty officers, thinking, as 'twas so short a run into port, there was no great risk of their meeting any Yankee cruiser. Ben knew very well there was no time to lose, and laid his plans with the doctor for re-taking the vessel that very night. They apprehended but little trouble from the seamen, who were most of them pressed men; but there were three marines to be got rid of,—one on the forecastle, and one at each gangway, and armed to the teeth. The doctor secured the key of the arm-chest as soon after twelve o'clock as the watch, who came below, were well asleep. Ben took off the splints and bandages, and crawling out of his hammock, wrenched the handcuffs from the wrists of eight of his men."

"Who did he let loose?" said Uncle Isaac; "anybody I know?"

"Yes; John Strout, and black Cæsar, who was the strongest man in the vessel, except Ben."

"I knew him; he was a slave to Seth Valentine, and he gave him his liberty when the war broke out."

"And Calvin Merrithew, who was almost as stout; and Ed Griffin, brother to Joe, who was killed afterwards, with Jack Manley, in the Lee privateer. The rest of 'em didn't belong round here."

"I heard something about it at the time, but never heard the particulars. But were not these sailors armed?"

"No; they don't allow sailors arms when about their duty; the marines do all the guard duty; the sailors are only armed in time of action. The doctor had a dog, who got the end of his tail jammed off a day or two before, under the truck of a gun carriage. The men, for deviltry, would touch it, to make him sing out; he got so at last, that if anybody pointed at it he would howl. They resolved to make the howl of the dog, which was too common to attract attention, a signal for action. They dressed themselves in the hats and coats of the watch who had turned in, that they might be taken in the dark for men-o'-war's-men. Cæsar went up the main hatch, passed the sentry on the forecastle, and went into the head. As 'twas nothing uncommon for men to come up in the night, the marine took no notice of 'em. Merrithew, Ed Griffin, and another, lay at the steps of the main hatch, watching the marine there; Ben, John Strout, and the others at the after hatch. The doctor, who went and came without question, pinched the dog's tail, who instantly began to howl. Cæsar felled the marine with a blow of his fist, and flung him overboard; Merrithew, rushing upon the marine at the hatchway, whose attention was occupied with the noise on the forecastle, flung him head foremost into the hold, while the others put on the hatches and barred them down. In the mean time Ben, rushing upon the sentry in the gangway, flung him against the lieutenant, who was pacing the deck, with such force as to fell him senseless on the planks, while the doctor locked the cabin doors, and the rest barred down the after hatches, then, seizing the boarding-pikes that were lashed to the main boom, joined their comrades. The seamen made little or no resistance. A terrible noise and swearing were now heard aft; the prize captain, having got up on the cabin table, with his head out of the skylight, was screaming to know why the doors were fastened, and what was the matter.

"'Come out here and see, my little man,' said Ben, reaching down, and taking him by both ears, he pulled him through the skylight, and set him astride a gun.

"'Who are you?' exclaimed the astonished commander.

"'This,' said the doctor, 'is the man with the broken leg; he's got well; I never had a patient mend so rapidly.'"

"I don't think that was very civil treatment for a prisoner of war," said Uncle Isaac.

"It was tit for tat," said Captain Rhines. "In the first of the war the British frigates used to run our privateers down, and destroy all hands, and starve and maltreat our prisoners in their hulks; but they got more civil in the last of it. I tell you, Ben would stick a mast into Elm Island, and sail it to Boston, if he undertook it."

CHAPTER XXIII.

PETE, IN QUEST OF REVENGE, COMES TO GRIEF.

"SAM HADLOCK," said his mother, "they say Ben's gone to Boston on a raft, all alone. I don't believe it; but go right over and see what it all means, and take Sally's hens on."

Sam arrived at Elm Island about dusk, with the hens and a crower. The first thing a rooster does, upon finding himself in a strange place, is to flap his wings and crow, in order that it may be known he is round. The next morning, as the daylight shone in between the logs of the hovel, he raised his cry of defiance to all things in general, and everybody in particular.

Now, although the squawks had been in possession of the island from time immemorial, they had never heard a rooster crow, or even seen one. The instant that shrill, defiant voice rose on the morning air, saying, "I'm somebody; who are you?" every squawk on the island uttered his loudest yell. This startled the herons and fish-hawks; the crows joined the chorus, and Sailor exerted his lungs to the utmost. Sally woke up in alarm, and was for some time unable to account for the terrible uproar. It was a week before the Elmites would permit the rooster to crow, or a hen to cackle, in peace. The moment he attempted it, the whole community combined to drown his voice, and rebuke his presumption; but, after a while, they began to recognize him as an adopted citizen of that of which they had so long been the sole occupants. It was laughable to see with what gravity they would cluster on the trees, at the edge of the woods near the house, and, with their keen eyes, stare at him and his dames. Now and then a great blue heron would sail lazily overhead, when, the cock raising the cry of alarm, all would scud for the barn; but they learned, after a while, that none of the original inhabitants were to be feared, except the eagles.

The next morning, after the arrival of the hens, a calf, bright red, with a white star in his forehead, and white on his fore legs and the end of his tail, made his appearance.

Sally was delighted; the birth of the calf opened a prospect not only of milk, of which they had been deprived for two months, but of butter. It was also the first domestic animal that had been born on the island; besides, there are so many pleasant memories of childhood connected with a "bossy," that it seemed a great affair to Sally in her lonely situation. She scarcely ever came in from the barn but her sleeves were all chewed up, in consequence of stopping to pet the calf.

"How much it seems like home," said she to Joe, "to have a calf to pet, and hear it crying for the cow! to hear a rooster crow, and hens cackle, and have eggs to hunt after! I used to think, when I first came on here, it would be music to hear a pig squeal."

"I can give you music," said Joe, and set up a cry so much like that of a pig in his last agonies, that Sally was glad to stop her ears. He then began to make a noise like a calf in trouble, which soon brought the mother running from the woods, where she had been browsing upon maples that Joe had cut down for her.

Peter Clash embraced the first opportunity in the spring to ship in a fishing vessel, being in mortal fear of Uncle Isaac, who, Joe Griffin had told him, had Indian blood in him, and would carry him into the woods and roast him alive, as he had been taught to do among the Indians. But he was determined, before he departed, to revenge himself upon Uncle Isaac, and inflict some injury upon John Rhines. He hated John, although he had never injured him, because he was a good boy, and Uncle Isaac and everybody liked him. Although two years older, he feared to attack him. He talked with the boys who were most under his influence, and by ingenious falsehoods contrived to prejudice them against him, by possessing them with the idea that John helped Uncle Isaac set the trap, and was in the bushes with him watching them when it sprung.

"I hate him, too," said Jack Godsoe, whose mind Pete had completely warped to his own interest, and who was also older than John, and a smart, resolute boy.

"He thinks he's too good to play with us, because his father is captain, and lives in a big house, and because he goes with Uncle Isaac; I hate him; let's lick him, and take some of that grand feeling out of him."

They seated themselves on the beach, under a great willow that hung over the bank, in earnest consultations as to the best means of revenging themselves upon Uncle Isaac. Jack proposed they should pull up his corn.

"That," said Fred Williams, "is too much work, and he could plant it over again."

"Let us put his sheep in the well," said Sam Smikes.

"It's too near the house," said Pete; "we shall be caught; besides, it wouldn't be bad enough for the 'old cuss;' he could get them out, and would save the wool and the pelts, for they are not sheared. O! I'll tell you what we'll do; we'll kill his apple trees."

Uncle Isaac had an orchard in full bearing, that he valued very highly, having, at a great deal of labor and expense, obtained the trees of the Rev. Samuel Deane, of Portland. They were most of them grafted,—a rare thing in those parts at that day,—as Dr. Deane understood the art and mystery of grafting. They determined to girdle all these trees, which would be a most severe blow to Uncle Isaac, as he had watched over them for twenty years; and they were now in full bearing, having been planted on a burn among the ashes, and had thriven apace in the new, strong soil. It could also be accomplished without risk of detection, as the orchard was at a distance from the house. The meanness of the act seemed greater, because of the generous nature of the owner, who was not a niggard of his fruit, but gave the boys all the apples and cider they wanted. The fact that this villanous plan was eagerly assented to by the rest, shows to what an extent the example and influence of Pete had corrupted these boys. They thought themselves secure from interruptions, as they commanded from the place where they sat a view of the whole beach, and, becoming excited, talked in a louder tone than they were aware of.

"I'll set a trap for him that will make him ache as much as his trap did me," said Pete, chuckling. But doubtful things are uncertain.

John's mother had sent him on that morning after some willow bark, to color with. He directed his steps to the great willow, and coming upon the party before they were aware of it, heard the latter part of their conversation. Pete espied him, and jumping up, in a pleasant tone invited him to come down among them, when John, who had not heard that portion of the consultation which related to himself, complied: they all, at a wink from Pete, surrounded him, who now thought proper to change his tone.

"You heard what we were saying about?" he inquired, pointing in the direction of Uncle Isaac's.

"Yes."

"And you'll tell him of it?"

"Yes."

"Ain't that just what I told you?" said he, turning to the other boys; "just such a mean, low-lived fellow as he is; go and peach on his playmates!"

"I should think if anything was mean, it was barking a man's apple trees in the night."

Now, Pete was more anxious to bark the apple trees than he was to lick John; so he replied,—

"Well, if we will promise to give it up, will you promise to say nothing about it?"

Pete's design in this was to prevent Uncle Isaac being put on his guard, to bark the trees that night, and go off the next morning, leaving the other boys to take the consequences. He knew if John gave his word he'd keep it. But John fathomed their design; and although *they* could trust *him*, *he* would not trust *them*, and refused.

At this Pete said, "You're a mean fellow; I've owed you a hiding this long time, and now you'll get it."

"You can't begin to do it."

"We all can," cried Jack.

John, seeing there was no help for it, determined to have the first blow, and before the words were fairly out of Jack's mouth, knocked him down; but as the ground was descending, and the sand afforded poor footing, he fell forward with the force of his own blow, and came upon one knee. They all piled on top, but John threw them off. By a well-directed blow he sent Fred yelling from the conflict, and would have gained his feet and handled the whole of them, had not Jack recovered, and, catching him by the hair, pulled him down again.

"Now," cried Pete, as cruel as he was cowardly, "let's lick him within an inch of his life."

Finding he was to receive no quarter, John began to shout for aid. Tige was sleeping in the sun before the door, as dogs always sleep, with one ear open. The instant he heard the cry, he got up, stretched himself, gaped, and listened. It was repeated. He leaped the front yard fence at a bound, and in a moment was running full speed in the direction of the noise. Captain Rhines, who recognized John's voice, followed him. A narrow path led down the bank to the beach, where the scuffle was going on, and which was hard trodden and polished by the frequent tramping of the boys, who resorted there to swing on the great willow, whose limbs hung over the beach, and to make whistles. So headlong was the speed of the dog, that, his feet slipping upon the smooth path, he turned a complete somerset from the top to the bottom of the bank, and came down upon his back among these little fiends, while employed in their work of torture, thus affording them a moment's respite while he was picking himself up. With all the speed the fear of instant death could inspire, they fled along the beach, with the exception of Smike, who, with great presence of mind, catching a limb of the willow, was in a few moments among its topmost branches, screaming with all his might. Pete was the hindmost. With a horrible growl, Tige sprung upon him and crushed him to the earth. He bit through both his hands, with which he strove to defend his throat, tore away half of his chin, and, taking him by the back, shook him as he would a woodchuck.

The dog now pursued Fred, whom he bit through both thighs and arms, and, as the others were out of sight, would have killed him, had not John compelled him to desist by cramming his cap into his mouth, and coaxing and scolding him.

The Newfoundland dog is very slow to wrath, but ferocious enough when once aroused. Tige's rugged temper, excited by the strongest possible provocation,—injury to the person of his friend,—was now thoroughly up; his eyes were green with rage, his lips covered with foam; his great tearing teeth stood out, and every hair on his body was erect.

As Captain Rhines came up, the blood was spirting in jets from Fred's right leg. "God o' mercy!" cried he, "the arter is cut;" and, clapping his thumb on the place, stopped the flow of blood in a moment.

"John," cried he, "take off my garter and put it twice round his leg, above the bite, and tie the ends together."

John did as he was directed.

"Now get a stick and twist it."

John twisted.

"Twist harder; twist with all your might. Now run to Dr. Ricker's, and tell him to come to our house with tools to tie an arter, as quick as he can."

"Will he die, father?"

"No; I hope not; but he would have been dead in two minutes more, if I had not stopped that blood."

He now took the boy in his arms, and carried him to his own house, while Tige lay down at the foot of the willow to keep watch of Smike.

The doctor said that the boy must not be moved; and his mother came to take care of him. John now went down, called off Tige, and liberated Smike from the tree.

"John," said the captain, after the excitement was over, "did you set the dog on those boys?"

"No, father; they had me down on the ground, beating me; I screamed for help, and Tige came and went right at 'em. I got him off of Fred as soon as I could, but he wouldn't mind me; and he was so savage I was afraid of him myself."

"What did they beat you for?"

"They were all sitting on the beach, planning out to pull Uncle Isaac's corn up, throw his sheep in the well, and girdle his apple trees; because I overheard 'em, and wouldn't promise not to tell him, they pitched into me. I believe I could have whipped the whole of them, if I hadn't fell down."

"I wouldn't have believed that of boys raised round here; it's a pity Tige hadn't finished that Pete; he was at the bottom of it."

When Pete recovered from his wounds he left the place. The parents of the others gave them a severe whipping, in consequence of which Jack Godsoe ran away from home, but the others left off their tricks, and became steady, industrious boys.

"On deck there!" cried Captain Rhines, from the roof of the house, where he was stopping a leak.

"What is it, father?" said John.

"Tell your mother Ben has just come round Birch Point in his canoe, and is going across to the island; I guess he wants to kiss Sally, for he's making the canoe go through the water like blazes."

The next morning they saw him coming off in the canoe.

"Well, Ben," said his father, after the greeting had passed, "when I was young, folks didn't go to sea without bidding their folks good by. Now, give an account of yourself."

Ben, who knew his father, old sailor like, would want to know the details of the passage, said, "By twelve o'clock the first night I was up with Purpooduck, right off the pitch of the cape; the wind was very strong and steady from sunrise till midnight."

"I know it was; for I was up watching it."

"It then died away to a flat calm; and as the flood tide was drifting me into Portland Sound, I anchored and made a fire."

"What on?"

"A flat stone I carried; made a cup of tea, and slept till daylight, when the wind, blowing the smoke in my face, woke me. The wind held, and plenty of it. I run her all day and all night, and by eight o'clock the next morning I was up with Cape Ann, when it fell calm. It was flood tide; I went to sleep and let her drift. When I woke up, the tide had carried me, with a little air of wind there was, up to East Point; and, in the course of the day and night, I tied her to Long Wharf, Boston—not much sorry."

"What did Mr. Welch say?"

"He was somewhat astonished. There were hundreds of people on the wharf to look at me or the raft, I don't know which. I got there in a good time. There were a great many vessels there, from Europe, after spars—especially big masts. I sold enough to pay for half the island, and I haven't cleared a quarter of it; but that is not the best of it."

"I should think that was good enough; what can be any better?"

"I sold all the timber that I used to confine the raft (and that was full of holes) for wharf stuff—the cable, sail, everything but the compass, canoe, and tea-kettle. I got a chance to pilot a French ship, that was bound to Portland for lumber and horses, and got a round price for it. They took the canoe on the ship's deck. In Portland I found a schooner bound to Nova Scotia; they took me to Gull Rock, and I rowed home. Thus I got mighty good pay for doing my own work."

"Well, Ben, at that rate I would cut every stick off the island, and sell the island for whatever anybody, who is fool enough to live there, will give, and come on to the main land, and buy a place among folks."

"Not yet, father; that is, if Sally likes to live there. I wouldn't swap it for the best place and house in town."

Ben was now reduced to a single yoke of oxen, as those he had hired were needed at home, and without them he could not handle spars, which must be hauled some distance; but on the eastern side of the island was a place where the rocks, undermined by the frosts and sea, had fallen into the water. He cut the trees around it into mill-logs that were not fit for spars, rolled them down the chasm into the water, towed them to the mill, bringing back the boards, and sticking them up on the shore to season. Thus they worked all through the summer, despite of black flies and mosquitos.

They then cut a lot of cedar, and piled it up to dry with the boards.

"What are you going to do with all this cedar?" said Joe; "and why don't you sell your boards at the mill, instead of bringing them back here?"

"I won't tell you," said Ben; "so you needn't ask me."

In September, Joe, who had agreed to go on a fishing trip with John Strout, left, and Ben was once more alone.

Let us now see how matters are going with Fred, who, by fright, wounds, loss of blood, and remorse of conscience, was brought well nigh to death's door. For a long time he was so reduced, and in such a state of stupor, as not to know where he was; but as he regained strength and perception, it mortified and stung him to the quick to find himself in the house, and the object of care and solicitude to those whom he had so recently injured; for, notwithstanding the mean, cowardly treatment John had received from Fred, he was unremitting in his attentions to him,—sleeping in the same room, and ministering to all his wants. It is wonderful to what lengths a boy of a naturally kind and generous nature may be induced to go in wickedness,—and mean wickedness, too,—through the influence of evil examples and companionship.

Such a boy was Fred; and this kind treatment was perfect torture. At length he could bear it no longer; but upon a night when he had been feverish and very restless, and John had been up great part of the night, bathing his head, and giving him drink and medicines, he said, while his voice was choked with sobs, "O, John, I don't deserve all this kindness at your hands; I don't see how I could ever have gone in with that miserable Pete, and those boys, to hurt you. If I ever get well, I'll be a better boy, and try to show you and your folks that I am not ungrateful."

He had made promises of amendment to John before, especially when suffering under the smart of the fish-hook. They came from the lips then—a repentance in view of consequences; but Tige's teeth went deeper than the fish-hook, and this time they came from the heart.

Little Fannie now came down to see her brother. The first thing she did, upon entering the house, was to put both arms round Tige's neck, and tell him he shouldn't be whipped if he did do naughty things, for Captain Rhines said so.

Fred's father was a stern, passionate man, who did not secure the affections of his children. His mother was a fretful, teasing woman; thought she had to work harder, and had more to try her than anybody else in the world; didn't see what she had so many children for; when the window was down she wanted it up, and when it was up she wanted it down; was never suited. She was a great deal more inclined to scold her children for doing wrong, than to praise them for doing well. The doctor said Fred would never get well, if his mother took care of him, she kept such a fuss, and made him uneasy; so Mrs. Rhines told her there were a good many of them, and they could take care of him as well as not, and had plenty of room; that she had a great family, with much to do, and young children; their dog did the harm, and they would take care of him.

As Fred began to mend, Mrs. Rhines would take her work and sit down by him in the afternoon, and talk with him as she did with her own children; in her kind, motherly way, tell him of the results of vice, and the inducements to a virtuous course; and, as the tears ran down his cheeks, wiped them away, soothing and encouraging him, till the boy's inmost soul responded to her teachings. His eyes would light up with satisfaction when he saw her take her knitting work to sit by his bedside.

Not long after Fred had given vent to his feelings, John, meeting Uncle Isaac on the beach, said to him, "I believe Fred would be right glad to see you, but don't like to say so."

"Well, I'll happen in."

So he happened in. What passed between them was never known; but the next day Fred said to John, "Uncle Isaac's a good man—ain't he?"

"Good! He's the goodest man that ever was."

Not many days after he happened in again, when Fred said to him, "I have an uncle in Salem that's a tanner and shoemaker. He and I were always great friends; he wants me to come and live with him, and learn the trade. Father has said a great many times that I am such a bad boy, and plague him so much, that he should be glad if I was there. I've been thinking while on this bed, that since I have got such a bad name round here, it would be a good thing to go where nobody knows me, or what I have done, and begin brand fire new."

"The tanner's trade is a first-rate one, and I should like to have you learn it; but the place where you have lost your character, Fred, is the very place to get it again. There was a man lived in Rowley, who was accused of stealing a sheep. He said he wouldn't stay in a place where he was so slandered, and moved to Newbury. He had not been there a fortnight when the report came that he had stolen three sheep when he lived in Rowley, and he moved back again."

"But everybody will scorn me; and when I go to school the boys will twit me of it, and holler after me when I go along the road."

"No boy or man, whose opinion is worth minding, will do it when they see you mean to mend; besides, you ought to be willing to suffer some mortification on account of the sorrow you have caused your parents and friends, and for all the mischief you have done, and meant to do."

"That is true; and I *am* willing they may say or do what they like; I'll *face* it."

"That's right; that's bravely spoken," said Captain Rhines, laying his great hand upon the pale forehead of the sick boy; "you'll live it down, and be thought more of for it. You see, my son, building character is just like building a vessel. We build a vessel model, fasten, spar, and rig her the best we know how, and *think* she'll prove serviceable; still we don't know that. But when she's made a winter passage across the western ocean, and the captain writes home that she is tight, and sails and works well in all weathers, then you see that vessel's got a character; sailors like to go in her, and merchants like to put freight in her. That will be the way with you; people will say there's good stuff at bottom in that boy; he's been through the mill."

"But," said the poor boy, "who will believe that I'm going to be a good boy? and who will go with me at the first of it, while I'm proving myself?"

"John will go with you, and our girls."

"I," said Uncle Isaac, "will get Henry Griffin to go with you. Pete tried to get hold of him, but he didn't make out. I'll get him to come down and see you to-morrow."

When the cool weather came on, Fred gained strength, went to school, and began to help his father in the mill.

It was remarkable how soon people began to notice the change in him, and to say, "What a smart boy Fred Williams is getting to be! and how much help he is to his father!" He could not have been placed in a better position to have his light shine, than in a mill, where everybody in the whole town came, and were convinced of the shrewd wisdom of Uncle Isaac's declaration, that the place to look for a thing was where you lost it; the place to regain confidence, where you had forfeited it.

Our readers will recollect the longing for some kindred spirit near his own age, which John expressed to his mother. That desire was now to be gratified in a most wonderful manner, as will be seen in the next volume of "Elm Island Stories," entitled CHARLIE BELL, THE WAIF OF ELM ISLAND; and we cannot help thinking it must have been as a reward for his remarkable conduct towards Fred.